THE NIGHT I
DISAPPEARED

Julie Reece Deaver

Simon Pulse

New York · London · Toronto

Sydney · Singapore

First Simon Pulse edition May 2002

Text copyright © 2002 by Julie Reece Deaver

SIMON PULSE
An imprint of Simon & Schuster
Children's Publishing Division
1230 Avenue of the Americas
New York, NY 10020

Designed by Interrobang Design Studio
The text of this book was set in Sabon.

Printed in the United States of America
10 9

Library of Congress Control Number: 2001096787
ISBN 0-7434-3979-1

"I'll be right back," I say, heading for my bed-room. "I want to get my backpack . . ."

It's not just the backpack I need. I need to sit down on the bed and be quiet a minute. I need to stop shaking. I need to forget that horrendous crime-scene photograph. I need . . .

Webb stands on the bike trail down by the bay. It's almost dusk now, and the chilly fog hazes up a purple-pink sunset.

"Cold, Jamie!" He shouts to me. "You picked a hell of a night to come back for a visit. Starting to rain, too."

"Wow, what a greeting," I shout back, and he laughs and holds out his hand. I love the way our hands fit together—like they were made for each other. A perfect match.

"Jamie?" Morgan says. "What's wrong? Are you okay? Jamie?"

I can barely hear her; she's too far away. I'm guessing she's just walked into my room and dis-covered I've disappeared, pulled a vanishing act. She must be plenty scared, but what can I do about it from here? I turn away from the faint sound of her voice and follow Webb down to the water.

To Jeffery Deaver, creator of the Lincoln Rhyme novels, who is not only the best writer I know, but is also the big brother I was lucky enough to grow up with.

And special thanks to Sharyn November, for generously giving so much of her time and extraordinary talent to this project.

THE NIGHT I DISAPPEARED

* PART ONE *

PART ONE

1

THE GIRLS' WASHROOM AT SCHOOL CAN be a scary place. That's the thought that occurs to me as I hurry inside to check my hair before I cut seventh period. A gaggle of cheerleaders—The Stevens Six, I call them—stands at the mirror chattering as they whip their mascara wands into a frenzied overdrive in an effort to improve upon their already perfect reflections. This is serious business for them: The end-of-the-year honors assembly is just minutes away, and it's vital that they look their best. It gets deadly quiet as I take a place at the mirror. The cheerleaders are just six out of billions of other people on this planet who are not my friends. I only have one friend, and he's waiting for me down at the beach.

"Hey, Jamie," one of them—Sara—says to me. "I saw your mom interviewed on the news last night. Wow, what's it like to have a mother who's such a famous lawyer?"

I shrug; look through my backpack for my hairbrush.

"They said she's going to Chicago to defend that rich girl—what's her name—Sally Renfro, the girl who killed her stepfather."

I concentrate on my hair. It looks terrible today. I make a mental note to switch my brand of shampoo.

"Your mom seemed so together," Sara says. "I was really surprised."

I turn to look at her. "What exactly is your point, Sara?"

"Well, Jamie, if you really want to know, I was just wondering what it's like for your mom—this successful, high-powered attorney type—to have a daughter who's such a major embarrassment, who's flunking out of Stevens because she's so—"

"—spacey," one of her friends says, and they all laugh.

Sara's open makeup kit is poised on the edge of the sink. It doesn't take much effort to bump into it on my way out of the washroom. It's pretty satisfying to glance back and see that shocked expression on her face as the plastic containers of eyeshadow, mascara, lipstick, and blush hit the floor and scatter across the tile.

Sara's right about me, I think, as I sneak out of the building and run down to the beach. She's trying to tell me in her own special way that I'm not Stevens material. I can't argue with that. I don't fit in there, or anywhere, really. I've tried to explain this to my mother a few hundred times but have not had much success.

"Jamie," she'll say, "Stevens is one of the best private schools in California, and you know it.

You're talented in a lot of things—music, art, writing—but you need a strong academic foundation so you can *do* something with those talents. . . ."

I have heard The Speech so many times, I can tune her out at the same time I'm nodding and looking like I'm agreeing with her.

I don't really care if I don't belong at Stevens, as long as I belong to someone, and I do, and there he is, kicking at the purple ice plant that dots the bay.

"Webb!" I yell, and he turns around and smiles. The fog rolling off the bay has made his blond hair wild and frizzy.

"Hey, you," he says, sliding his arms around me. My knees go weak, but I know he won't let me fall. "I was afraid I wouldn't see you before I left on my trip. . . ." He bends down and peeks at my face. "Another wonderful day at school, huh?"

"I've been going to that snake pit for three years, and this semester has been the worst. Did I tell you I flunked my academic probation? They're making me repeat part of my junior year in the fall."

"A snobby prep school isn't the right place for you, Jamie."

"I'm stuck there. My mom wants me to go to Stevens, which I hate, so I can get into an Ivy League college, which I don't care about."

He laughs. "Hang in there. You only have a couple of days before summer vacation starts."

"Believe me, I'm counting the milliseconds."

He takes my hand, and we climb down the rocks

to Otter Cove. We have this sanctuary all to ourselves today—our own private little piece of California. I love it here, this quiet cove where we can be alone together and watch the otters chase each other through the kelp. I sit on a giant rock; Webb settles right behind me like we're on a toboggan sled.

"So tell me how I'm supposed to get along without you," I say. "I mean, you and I haven't been separated since the night we met. Now we're both going away for the summer and—I'm not kidding, Webb. I don't think I can handle a solo kind of life."

I feel his hands on my hair, gently gathering it back into a ponytail. "Jamie."

"What?"

"A few months apart isn't going to change anything for us."

"I'm not so sure."

"Jamie. Repeat after me: Nothing is going to change for us this summer."

I sigh. "Nothing is going to change for us this summer—I hope."

"What an optimist. You *could* look on this summer as an adventure, you know. You'll probably have a blast in Chicago."

"Yeah, I really can't wait to be alone in some strange city while my mom's locked up in a courtroom all day defending some girl who killed her stepfather." I lean back against him. "I wish I could go with you this summer."

"I just don't see you as the type who'd like back-packing through Europe, Jamie. No five-star hotels, no television, no room service, no indoor plumbing—"

"Well, you're right. I really am addicted to indoor plumbing." I rest my chin on my knees. "My dad backpacked through Europe one summer, though, my mom says, and had the time of his life."

"You never talk much about your dad."

"He died in a boating accident out on the bay when I was like three and a half or something; I don't really remember him. They met in law school, my mom and dad, and I guess he was just as driven about his career as my mom is about hers."

"Your mom's pretty amazing. I saw her talking about the Renfro trial on the news last night. Very impressive."

"Did you see that clip they showed of Sally Renfro being taken to jail in handcuffs and leg shackles? It was just chilling. I can't stop thinking of what it must be like for her; what she must be feeling."

"At least she has one of the best attorneys in the country—"

"Yeah. Maybe I'm being selfish, but I *hate* it when my mom's involved in a high-profile trial like this. The reporters camp out on the front yard and shove their microphones into our faces the minute we walk out the door."

We're quiet a minute, watching the otters twist and tumble and spin in a show of aquatic gymnastics.

They're so comical we both laugh, a momentary distraction from what I've been dreading.

I know it's here, though, when Webb stretches his arms out in front of me and checks his watch. "I never noticed that before," I say, running my fingers along a zigzag-shaped scar near his elbow. "How'd it happen?"

"Playing football in the park one afternoon with my buddies. You'll have to come watch one of our games sometime. You'll lose all respect for me once you see what a truly horrible athlete I am." He stands and pulls me to my feet. "It's time, Jamie. My plane leaves at six, and I still have to pick up my paycheck from the construction job I worked last week. I need all the money I can get for my great European adventure."

It's treacherous climbing up the wet rocks, but Webb holds my hand firmly, and before I know it, we're safely out of the cove.

"This separation wouldn't be so hard on me if we could at least stay in touch with each other through E-mail or something."

"Jamie, I'm going to be camping. *Camping*. As in no electricity, no internet connection, no phones, no fax, no FedEx, no—"

"All right, all right, I get the picture."

"Doesn't mean I won't be thinking of you, though."

"I can't even *begin* to tell you how much that means to me, Webb."

He leans his forehead against mine. "You know what you don't do well? Sarcasm."

"I'm entitled to behave any way I want. I've got a broken heart."

"That's better. Winsome becomes you."

"I like being winsome. It sounds romantic, somehow."

He throws his arm around my shoulder, and we walk down to the bike trail, the place where we'll say good-bye. So. This is it.

"Do you ever think about the night we met?" I ask. "Do you even remember it?"

He looks at me. "Oh. I get it. I'm supposed to reminisce now, right?"

"If you can."

"Jamie, I'm hurt. Your lack of faith in me is—"

"You don't remember. Admit it."

"You were nine years old," he says. The tone in his voice is just right: warm and low. "And one night, while I was taking a shortcut through the woods, I noticed you all alone in the park. You were scared and crying because your baseball game had been over for hours and there was some mix-up with your ride home. No one had come to pick you up."

"You told me not to worry. You told me you'd look after me, remember?"

"I remember. I just didn't know at the time it would end up being my life's work."

"Not funny!" I say, pretending to jab him in

the ribs with my elbow. "God, you have to ruin a perfect moment . . ."

He scoops a shell off the beach and presses it into my hand. "Here," he says. "Something to remind you of California while you're gone." I turn the cracked sand dollar over in my hand. It's thin and fragile and could crumble very easily. I slip it into my pocket so I won't drop it.

"Have a good summer," he whispers, giving me a hug. I think I was hoping for more than that. I watch as he runs across the bike trail and heads for home. We started out as acquaintances, then became friends, and now . . . well, I look at him differently now than as just a friend, that's for sure. I wonder if it's the same for him. It's the ultimate case of bad timing, I think, being separated from him just as things might be growing more serious between us.

I turn around and walk home. It's really a depressing thought: summer without Webb. I wish we could go on seeing each other like we have since the night we met—that night he stepped out of the woods and into my life when I was only nine years old.

2

IT'S LIKE BEING TRANSPORTED TO OZ.
I mean, this morning I was packing my suitcase in a
foggy little California village, and this evening here
I am in Chicago, standing on the balcony of our
new apartment, looking out at a concrete maze of
steel-and-glass skyscrapers. The sublet is pretty
cool, actually: Good-sized bedrooms overlook a
garden courtyard, and there's a sunny kitchen
where I can whip up some of my gourmet special-
ties. There's even a bicycle in the entry hall with a
Post-it note stuck on the handlebars that says: FEEL
FREE TO RIDE ME. I wonder what it'd be like to
zoom through the streets on that bike and explore
the city.

"Jamie?" my mother calls from the living room.
"Have you seen my briefcase? I need it for my meeting tonight. I'll kill myself if I left it on the plane."

"It's in the kitchen."

"I just looked there."

"It's on the counter."

"I don't see it."

I make my way around the stacks of legal files
Mom has piled on the living room floor. We've
only been in Chicago a few hours, and she's already

managed to turn the apartment we're subletting into some sort of law library.

"Are we going to have to live like this all summer?" I ask.

"Like what?" my mother says, slipping into her jacket. She's wearing her navy blue suit tonight. She looks good in blue and wears it a lot in court. "The files, you're talking about? Don't worry; I'm having most of them sent over to the law office I'll be using while we're here in Chicago."

Mom's briefcase peeks out from under a basket of fruit one of her lawyer friends sent over as a sort of housewarming gift.

"Your daughter may not be the world's best student," I say, "but she's a whiz at finding misplaced objects."

"Ah, what would I do without you?" she says, taking the briefcase from me. "I'm glad you brought up the subject of school, because—"

"Mom, come on, we just got here. Cut me a little slack, okay?"

"I wonder if it's too late to get you into some kind of summer school program around here—"

"Why? Why do I have to go to school at all this summer? Why can't I just explore the city or hang out in some quaint little coffeehouse somewhere and soak up the local culture?"

My mother tucks some papers into her briefcase. "Because, dear, I don't like the idea of your having a lot of unstructured time this summer."

"God, you make it sound like I'll join the nearest street gang and get my tongue pierced unless every minute of my day is planned."

"Jamie, let's not forget what happened this spring, all right?"

Here we go again.

"Do you have any idea how I felt when I got that call from your guidance counselor last month?" my mother asks, pausing only to swirl on her lipstick. "I never would have made so many trips to Chicago to prepare for the Renfro trial if I'd known how . . . how—"

"—irresponsible," I offer.

"Yes—thank you—how irresponsible you'd be while I was gone."

It's true. I was very irresponsible while my mom was in Chicago. I did some terrible things. I stopped studying and failed two important finals. I forged a note on my mom's office stationery so I could get out of school early each day and race down to the beach to meet Webb. He and I spent slow, delicious afternoons together. It was a living fairy tale while it lasted; then my mom came home from one of her Chicago trips just in time to get a call from my guidance counselor. Pandemonium. Meetings. I was put on academic probation, which I promptly failed.

"I honestly don't know what happened to you this spring," my mother is saying, and I'm momentarily disoriented. I have to adjust my thinking and concentrate on The Speech. "I sometimes wonder if I've been so busy preparing for the trial that you decided to do something crazy to get my attention—"

"Mom, please, we've been all through this—"

"If I hadn't already committed myself to the Renfro trial, we'd be back in California and you'd be in summer school at Stevens."

"So send me back home then. I already told you I didn't want to spend my summer here in Chicago."

"Let you live on your own this summer? I don't think so. You were on your own several times in the last few months, and it didn't work out too well, remember?"

"Mom, come on, didn't you ever get spring fever and cut class?"

"Spring fever? Jamie, do you realize what that little spring fever stunt cost you? You're going to have to repeat part of your junior year next term—"

"Mom, you're going to be late for your dinner meeting."

She looks at her watch. "All right," she says, frowning. "But we're not through with this." She slips her laptop computer into her briefcase. "I'm sure you'll want to go out this evening to do a bit of sightseeing, but don't go too far, all right? It'll be dark soon, and you don't know your way around yet. And I want you to be careful; this is Chicago, not Monterey, you know."

"Thanks for the geography lesson."

"I'm serious, Jamie."

"Mom, I'm not five years old. I'll be fine."

She heads for the door. "These meetings about the trial tend to last for hours, but I'll give you a call if I'm going to be very late."

I watch as she walks to the elevator. I know it's hard on her sometimes; being a mother and father and benevolent dictator, all rolled into one. She worries a lot because I'm growing up without a father, but I don't exactly feel deprived or anything. How could I? I was so little when he died that he's just a shadow figure to me. I don't remember him, not much; just the sound of his voice as he read to me: poetry, I think, and *Alice in Wonderland*.

Once Mom's elevator disappears, I hurry to my room and change into my grubbiest and most comfortable pair of jeans. It's time to get acquainted with this city, I've decided, and what better way to do it than on a bicycle? Before I start my tour of the town, though, I stop to take a look at the only thing I've bothered to unpack: my seashell collection from home. The pink, blue, pale brown and yellow shells from home sit on the windowsill in stark contrast to the urban backdrop beyond the glass. The shells aren't the beautiful burnished kind you find in souvenir shops back home; they're broken and misshapen—shells Webb and I have found on our walks on the beach. I pick up the little cracked sand dollar Webb gave me and slip it into my pocket. He's been in Europe for five days now. I wonder where he is exactly, what he's doing, who he's met.

Enough of this. I've promised myself I won't dwell on him. Well, not too much, anyway. There's a whole city out there to be explored, so I wheel the bicycle into the hall and ring for the elevator. I have a map of the downtown area in my back-pack, but it'll be more fun, I think, just to ride around the neighborhood and discover things on my own.

As soon as I'm out of our apartment building, I jump on the bike and fly out into the street. This place truly is Oz, and I'm Dorothy, trying to adjust to a strange new land. The city traffic is a bit daunting at first, but soon I'm going as fast as a professional bike messenger, zipping around cars and busses and trucks. The last time I flew down the street on a bike, Webb was the one doing the pedaling. I sat on the back of the bike with my arms wrapped around his waist and lis-tened to him complain as he struggled to pedal us uphill.

"This wouldn't be so hard if you were lighter," he told me.

"Aw, poor *baby*," I answered. "Only a little while till we start downhill, then it'll be a breeze."

"If we don't break our necks."

"Where's your sense of adventure?"

"Okay, Jamie," he said, pausing at the top of the hill, "you talk big, but let's see how brave you really are."

I found out quickly what a coward I was. He gave the bike a little push, then suddenly we were rocketing downhill, and I was clinging to him as tightly as I could.

"Scared?" he shouted.

"Hell, no."

"Liar."

He knew me too well. "Okay, so I'm lying! Webb, slow down!"

"C'mon, I thought you had such a great sense of adventure—"

"Not funny! Slow down!"

"Relax, Jamie," he said, gently easing us to a stop. He turned to grin at me. "I've told you a million times: I'd never let anything happen to you. . . ."

"Hey, what the hell is *wrong* with you!"

It takes me a second to realize I'm not back home with Webb, I'm here in Chicago, racing my bike through the rush hour traffic. I see the angry face of a cabdriver as I cut in front of him. "You're going to get yourself killed!" he shouts. "Watch where you're going!"

But there's no time to look at anything. My bike slams into a parked car, and in a split second

I'm airborne, tumbling over the handlebars—
   flying,
       flying
           through
               an
                   upside-
                       down
                           world.

3

I SIT QUIETLY IN THIS LITTLE CURTAINED-OFF section of the emergency room while the doctor, a scruffy young guy dressed in loose green surgical scrubs, wraps a bandage around my left arm and lectures me on the importance of bicycle safety.

"You're lucky you don't have a head injury," he says. "The paramedics said you really took a tumble off your bike. Next time, wear a helmet."

Next time? What next time? I completely mangled the bike, and it's not even mine. My mother will faint when she sees it—when she sees *me* and this nasty little gash on my arm, not to mention my banged-up knees, which hurt like hell and need something about a million times stronger than the Tylenol they gave me.

"How did it happen?" the doctor asks. "How did you lose control of your bike?"

"I don't know," I say, which isn't true, but there's no way I'm going to tell this total stranger I lost control of my bike because I was daydreaming about my sort-of boyfriend. "Are you finished?" I ask. "Can I go home now?"

"Not till your mother gets here," the doctor says, opening my chart and writing in it. "The nurses are still trying to reach her."

My mother will check her phone messages sometime during her business dinner and find out that I'm in the hospital and she'll have a heart attack. It's that simple. I hope someone at her table knows CPR.

"You'll probably be a little achy for a couple days," the doctor says, "but, as I mentioned, it could have been a lot worse. Sit tight, okay? I'm going to get your release forms ready and see if they've contacted your mother. . . ."

He pulls the curtains open and walks over to the nurses' station. There's a girl about my age a few feet away from my cubicle; she's doing her best to dodge all the activity in the ER and stay out of everyone's way. I wonder why she's here. She doesn't seem to be a patient, and she's no candy-striper, that's for sure: she's wearing a snazzy red cocktail dress. I'm thinking she's probably like the Stevens Six back home: popular. Snobby. But her eye catches mine, and she smiles.

"Hi," she says. "I'm doing my best not to get run over."

"Yeah, I can see that. I like your dress. Vera Wang, right?"

"Right . . . it's only mine for tonight, though. It's a temporary hand-me-down from my aunt."

"I'm wearing the latest in bike accident attire," I say, gesturing at my ripped shirt, and she laughs and wanders over to me. Up close, I can see how pretty she is. She has a real girl-next-door thing going for her: big blue eyes and a warm smile.

"Is that what happened to you?" she asks. "A bike accident?"

"I smashed into a parked car," I say, spinning the plastic hospital bracelet around my wrist. "God, I hate it here. I feel like some sort of banded bird. Tagged, so they can locate me after I migrate."

"This place is the worst, isn't it? It's so cold and clinical. So impersonal."

"How come you're here? Doesn't look like you've been in a bike accident or anything."

"I'm waiting for my aunt," she says, glancing across the ER. "That's her over there. We were on our way to a dinner party, and she was called in on an emergency."

"She's a doctor?"

"Yeah, a psychiatrist."

"I've never seen a doctor dressed like that before," I say. "Like she just stepped off the cover of *Vogue*. Slinky black dress, diamond earrings, three-inch heels, and she has a stethoscope draped around her neck. The whole thing makes sort of an interesting fashion statement, don't you think?"

"Saks Fifth Avenue Meets *General Hospital*," she says, and I laugh. I'm not used to kidding around like this with another girl. My humor-impaired peers at Stevens never include me in any kind of friendly banter. This is a new experience for me.

A young nurse steps inside my little cubicle. "Jamie? We finally reached your mother; she's on the way."

"Can I wait for her outside?"

"We can't release you till your mom gets here," the nurse says on her way out. "Your friend can stay with you, though, while you wait."

When the nurse is gone, the girl turns to me and says: "Well, as long as we're friends, I guess I should introduce myself. I'm Morgan Hackett. And you're Jamie—"

"Tessman," I say, and she gets that lightbulb-over-the-head-look you see in cartoons.

"Tessman? Are you related to the lawyer on the Renfro trial?"

"Yeah, that's my mom. She's defending Sally Renfro."

"Really?" She pulls up a stool and sits down. "You're from California, then, right? They did a profile of your mom on our local news last week."

"We're spending the summer here. Longer, maybe, depending on the length of the trial."

"It must be sort of exciting, isn't it," she asks, "to have a mom who's such a well-known attorney?"

That's almost the same question posed to me by one of the cheerleaders back home, but there are no hidden barbs in the question this time; she's just being friendly.

"Exciting? Sometimes, I guess. I don't think of her as being well known, though. She's just my mom, if you know what I mean, ragging on me to get good grades and stuff like that."

"I know what that's like," Morgan says. "I barely squeaked through my senior year last semester. It's a miracle I actually got into college."

"Where are you going?"

"I start at the Goodman Theater in the fall. It's a school here in the city."

"You're an actress?"

"Oh. Well, sort of. A beginning one. I've done a few workshops and plays around town. Nothing major yet."

"I was in a play once. In the third grade. I wanted to be Cinderella, but they made me one of the stupid mice."

"Well, you know the old showbiz saying: 'There are no small parts, only small rodents.'"

I can't help laughing. "You're the first person I've met tonight who's really talked to me. The doctors and nurses don't count. They swoop in, take a look at me, then swoop out again."

"Yeah, this place isn't exactly known for its warmth," she says. "Hey, do you want to get together once you've healed? I could show you around; give you a tour of the city."

"Thanks. I'd like that."

"I'll give you my number. . . ." She finds a pen in her purse and pulls a paper towel out of a dispenser on the wall. "These are my aunt's phone numbers, actually," she says, scribbling them down on the paper towel. "I'm staying with her this summer while my parents are in Europe."

"A friend of mine just left for Europe a few days ago. He's always wanted to backpack through France and Italy without indoor plumbing."

She makes a face. "Roughing it, you mean. No, thanks."

"I don't get it, either. Maybe it's a guy thing. I guess he wants to tame the land or something."

"The only thing I want to tame when I'm traveling is room service," Morgan says. "Is he your boyfriend?"

"Someday, maybe. We've just been really good friends for a long time."

"I had a friend like that. He and I were so close, we could practically read each other's minds."

"Are you still close to him?" I ask, and when she hesitates, I shake my head. "I'm sorry; it's none of my business."

"No, it's okay. It's just sort of a long story," she says, handing me the paper towel. "I'll be at the second number during the day. My aunt's setting up a new office downtown, and I'm going to be working for her."

The scruffy doctor bounces back into the cubicle. "Okay, Jamie, I want to take one more look at that arm."

"I'd better get out of here and give you some room," Morgan says. "Call me sometime, okay? I don't really have any friends in the city, and it'd be nice to have someone to get into trouble with this summer."

"I'll call you," I tell her. "Thanks."

Amazing. So maybe I'll have a friend this summer. And she and I seemed to be tuned to the same frequency, which has only happened to me with one other person, with Webb. Despite the bike accident, things are suddenly looking up a bit. I might not have to spend the summer by myself, something I was really dreading.

I guess I just really hate being alone.

4

MY MOTHER LISTENS CAREFULLY AS THE
ER doctor reassures her that even though I look
like I've been put through a meat grinder, I am rela-
tively unhurt. Mom seems unconvinced. She's spent
too much time as an attorney, I think, grilling witnesses in court and searching for hidden subtext in
everything they say.

It isn't until we're in the cab on the way home
that she relaxes enough to start cross-examining
me: "You decided to go for a bicycle ride at *night*?
What on earth were you thinking of?"

"It wasn't dark when I started out."

"When I got that message from the hospital"—
she turns to me—"and exactly how did you man-
age to slam into a parked car? Did some driver cut
you off?"

"I don't know. I guess I was daydreaming or
something and I wasn't paying attention to what I
was doing—"

"Not paying attention? You were out in all this
city traffic and you weren't paying attention?" She
sighs and slouches against the cracked vinyl of the
backseat. "Jamie . . ."

It's that sigh of disappointment that gets me. I

look away from her, out the window, as the city whooshes by. I'm close to crying, but I bite my lip and hold it in.

"I'm sorry," my mother says, after a moment. "You've had a terrible night; I shouldn't be picking on you."

"It's not like I set out to screw up all the time."

"Jamie, if I sound . . . I just get worried about you, that's all."

"I wrecked the bicycle, and it's not even mine."

"We'll replace the bike. The important thing is that you're all right."

I wonder what the cabdriver thinks of our conversation. He's probably used to hearing everything, though.

"Did I ruin your meeting tonight?" I ask.

"No, not at all . . . oh, that reminds me"—she pulls her cell phone out of her purse—"I have to give Drew a call; he's one of the other lawyers on the case."

"I think maybe I made a friend tonight," I say. "A girl about my age. Her aunt's a doctor at the hospital."

"Really?" my mom says, pressing the speed dial on her phone. "That's something I've always wanted for you. You don't seem to have any girlfriends back home."

"It's hard to make friends in that clique-ridden prison you call a school."

"Stevens is an excellent school, Jamie. You know that."

Yawn.

"It's important for you to do well there," my mom says. "You want to get into a good college, don't you?"

"No."

She starts to say something, then her attention's suddenly drawn to the phone. "Drew? Hi, it's me . . . no, she's fine. A little banged up, but fine. Did you get a chance to look at the Sachs file? Yes . . . that's what I thought, too. . . ."

I'm guessing Mom will be on the phone for the rest of the cab ride and all the way up to our apartment, and I'm right. Once we're inside, she kicks off her shoes and sits down at the kitchen table and continues talking with her friend Drew about the trial's opening statements, which are scheduled for tomorrow.

I don't see how she can do it: focus so completely on the trial after the scare I put her through earlier. Her powers of concentration are amazing—powers I absolutely did not inherit.

It turns out that the ER doc, though, has some pretty amazing powers of his own: He predicted the future with astonishing accuracy—every part of me hurts. I guess you can't morph into a human skyrocket and end up slamming into concrete and not expect to ache a little. I pop a couple of Tylenol into my mouth and chug them down with some stale ginger ale I find in the refrigerator.

"I'm going to bed," I whisper to my mom, and

she nods. I hear her wrapping up her phone call just as I crawl between the sheets.

"Jamie?" She comes into my room and leans against the door jamb. "I didn't mean to take so long," she says apologetically. "Can I get you anything?"

"No, I'm fine. I just want to get some sleep."

"It's been a hell of an evening, hasn't it? I'm off to bed, too. Good night."

"Night . . ."

I snap off the light and think about the bike accident. It's Webb's fault, it really is, for casting such a powerful spell over me that I crashed into a parked car while I was daydreaming about him. I wonder if he knows how he controls my heart even when we're not together. I wonder if it's the same for him; if he's thinking about me right now. I dread thinking of the days, weeks, months before I'll see him again.

It's going to be a long summer.

5

A COUPLE OF DAYS LATER I'M BASICALLY ache free and back to my old elastic self.

"You look a lot better this morning," my mom says as she hurries to get ready for court. "How do you feel?"

"Pretty good. I think I've recuperated enough to try taking on the city again." I'm in the kitchen, pouring coffee into my mom's commuter mug. "I'll get some groceries today so I can start doing some real cooking around here. What would you like for dinner?"

"Whatever you decide."

"Broiled salmon with sherried hollandaise?"

"Sounds wonderful. . . ." She's got her nose buried in her briefcase—probably a last-minute search for some vital document she'll need for court. "You'll be careful, though, won't you? I know you won't be on a bicycle this time, but I want you to pay attention to where you're going—"

"Mom, please, not another lecture."

"Jamie." I hear the strain in her voice. "After what happened the other night, you can't blame me for being concerned about you wandering around the city."

"I was just tired the other night, Mom. Jet lag or something. It's not going to happen again. Besides, I'm meeting Morgan for lunch, and I'm sure she'll show me around the city a little and make sure I don't get run over."

"Who's Morgan?"

"Morgan Hackett—the girl I met the other night in the emergency room. I told you about her, remember?"

She looks at me. "You did?"

"Yes . . . she was hanging around the ER waiting for her aunt and we got to talking—"

"I know. I remember now. The doctor's niece. I guess I've got my mind on the trial, but I'm sure you're all too aware of that."

"I think you're working *way* too hard," I tell her.

"No such thing with a murder case," my mom says, shutting her briefcase. She takes the mug of coffee from me. "I'll see you tonight; have a good day."

I can't get over it: Ever since I went flying off the Schwinn, my mom hasn't once brought up the idea of sticking me in summer school; probably another result of the tunnel vision she gets when she's focused on a trial. I don't mind that a bit, as long as it means I'm not stuck in a hot classroom somewhere conjugating irregular French verbs.

I'm supposed to meet Morgan at Marshall Field's, a downtown department store, but I'm hideous at decoding my Chicago map and take several wrong turns before I finally find State Street and see the building's antique clock Morgan described. As soon as I walk into the store I see her standing near the fragrance counter, getting spritzed by perfume snipers masquerading as attractive salesclerks.

"Jamie, hi," she says.

"Sorry I'm late. I got lost."

"You'll learn your way around in no time," she says. "Follow me; there's a great restaurant upstairs."

We take the elevator up to the seventh floor and wait to be seated in the Walnut Room, a grand upscale restaurant that's a far cry from the fried-food court at the mall back home. Morgan looks fantastic—she has a real sense of style, I can see: shirtless vest, low-rise corduroy pants, and cool-looking dangly earrings.

"So," she says, "did your mom freak when she saw you in the ER the other night?"

"In her own way, yeah. How'd you know?"

"I'm a veteran," she says. "I've been through a million of those mother-daughter moments."

"And yet you seem amazingly sane."

She laughs. "I'm really close to my mom, but there are times—well, take this summer, for example. We had this big disagreement because I didn't want to go to Europe with her and my dad; I wanted to stay here and work for my aunt and earn a little money for college. I want to contribute to my own future, you know? Be sort of independent. So my mom said she understood, but every time she calls from England, our phone conversations end with her saying something like, 'All right, if you'd really rather stay there in Chicago instead of having the once-in-a-lifetime experience of traveling through Europe with your father and me—'"

"Wow! Transatlantic guilt!"

"Hey, my mom's no amateur," Morgan says.

"Actually, my mom and I get along pretty well," I say. "But sometimes—like now, with the trial going on—things can get a little tense."

"Yeah, I can imagine. The trial's everywhere: You can't turn on the TV without seeing a reporter broadcasting from the courthouse."

"My mom calls it a tabloid story in search of the truth. I mean, here's Sally Renfro, this popular college student from one of the wealthiest families in Chicago, and one day the police show up on campus to arrest her for killing her stepfather. The media's jumped on the story and run with it; they're making her out to be some sort of cold-blooded killer, and it's just not true."

"The papers say that all the evidence points to her, though."

"My mom's going to argue it was self-defense. Justifiable homicide. Sally Renfro's stepfather had been abusing her for years. Yeah, just what you're thinking. *That* kind of abuse."

"God..."

The hostess shows us to a table, and a waiter zooms by and hands us menus and fills our water glasses. This room is beautiful and elegant—a white linen tablecloths and napkins and fresh-cut flowers type of place.

"My aunt and I come here for special occasions," Morgan says. "I thought it'd be a fun place for you to see; it's sort of a Chicago landmark."

"I'd love to bring my friend Webb to a place like this," I say. "Webb and I—he's the friend I was telling you about the other night, the one who's backpacking through Europe—anyway, we never go out to fancy restaurants; we usually just get something to eat at the concession stand by the beach."

"You must really miss him, huh?"

"We haven't been apart since the day we met. He's someone who's really easy to be with, you know?"

"You finish each other's sentences, right?"

"Yeah, right. I think of him as my soul mate."

"That's the way it was with my friend Jimmy," she says. "He was always there for me."

"It must have ended badly, though, from what you said the other night...." The look on Morgan's face—well, it's clear that what I've just said has caused her a lot of pain. I wish I could take it back.

"Oh," she says quietly. "Well, yeah. He was killed last winter by a drunk driver."

I'm so rattled at thinking about Morgan and

what happened to her friend that I don't know what to say.

She looks at me. "Jimmy and I were definitely soul mates. Like you and your friend Webb are. So I know what it's like to miss someone."

"If I'd known..." My words seem so clumsy. "I'm sorry I asked you about it."

"It's okay," she says. "I've just never really talked about it with anyone. To my family, I guess, but not to a friend."

"I've never had to go through anything like that. Well, my dad died, but I was like three and a half when it happened. I don't really remember him."

"Did your mom ever think about remarrying?"

"I don't think so. She's had a couple of boyfriends, but they never last very long. She's pretty consumed with her career right now."

"My aunt's a bit like that, I guess. She was pretty serious about her last boyfriend, though; they almost got married."

The waiter comes over to our table and asks if we're ready to order lunch, and Morgan says something to me about how famous the Walnut Room is for its chicken pot pie, so I order it, even though I don't really want that or anything else right now. I just can't shake the thought that the person sitting across from me has suffered a tremendous loss, yet she's going on with her life, making plans for college, for her future. . . . I wouldn't be able to go on at *all* if something happened to Webb.

I wouldn't *want* to go on, that's for sure.

"How did you handle it?" I ask, once the waiter is gone. "When your friend . . . well, how did you ever deal with something like that?"

"I didn't," she says. "I was beyond warped, believe me. I really went crazy."

"Literally, you mean? Did they put you in the hospital or something?"

"They probably would have, but I have an aunt who's a shrink, remember. It was like I kept falling deeper and deeper into a black hole, and she was the one who helped me find my way out of the darkness."

I can't even imagine what that kind of darkness would feel like.

"I didn't mean to get so serious," Morgan says. "I had this great welcome-to-Chicago speech planned for you, and all I've done is tell you my depressing life's story."

We're quiet for a minute. "I go to an exclusive prep school," I say, "and I don't have a single friend there. No one ever wants to tell me anything about their lives, and they sure as hell don't want to hear anything about mine."

Morgan nods. "On the outside looking in."

"Exactly."

"Yeah, I know what that's like. I didn't fit in at school, either."

"You seem—I don't know—too *cool* to be an outsider."

She laughs. "I've never really thought of myself as cool, but it's an adjective I can definitely live with."

"I really wasn't looking forward to coming here to Chicago," I say. "I mean, I'm not very good at making new friends."

"Well, that's changed now," Morgan says, picking up her glass. "Let's make a toast. You go first."

I pick up my glass. "To being outsiders."

"To being cool."

"To meeting someone I can get into trouble with."

"Something tells me we're going to have one hell of a summer together," she says, clinking her glass against mine. "Welcome to Chicago, Jamie."

6

From here I can see Webb, the moonlight soft around his wild blond hair. I love watching him run the track around the baseball field. He's fast. Graceful. I'm neither. Athletics is one of the few things we don't have in common.

"Webb!" I shout. "Hasn't it ever occurred to you that you'll never get anywhere if you keep running around in circles like that?"

He slows to a walk, looks around, and spots me sitting here on the bleachers. "You're doing comedy now?" he yells, trying to catch his breath. "Why don't you come over here, Jamie, and run a couple miles around this track. Then we'll see how funny you are."

"It's a tempting offer, Webb, but I think I'll pass on it."

"Coward." He walks over to the bleachers and I take his hand and pull him next to me. "What happened?" he asks, lightly touching the bandage on my arm.

"Bike accident," I say. "That's what I get for trying something aerobic."

"I think it's pretty obvious, Jamie, that you aren't safe out there in the world without me."

I look at him, astonished. "I hope you're kidding," I say, and he bursts out laughing.

"Well, duh," he says, starting to tickle me. "What do you think?"

Slam.

"Jamie?" my mom calls. "I'm home."

It takes me a couple of seconds to focus on my surroundings, to realize I'm not back home with Webb. He's in Europe, and I'm here in Chicago, standing in the kitchen of our sublet. Smoke is starting to float out of the oven and settle above me like a dark cloud.

"Jamie? Is something burning?"

I grab a pot holder and yank the broiler pan out of the oven and throw it into the sink. I turn the faucet on full blast, and there's the terrible hiss of steam as water hits the scorched metal.

"Something tells me we're eating out tonight," my mom says, walking into the kitchen. She flips on the exhaust fan over the stove, and the smoke is suddenly swallowed up into the ceiling.

"I don't know what happened." I look down at the lump of charcoal in the broiler pan that, until a few minutes ago, was a beautiful piece of sherried salmon. "I guess I didn't realize how long it had been under the broiler."

"It doesn't matter," my mom says. "We'll go out somewhere. There's that little Italian restaurant across the street—as long as we're back by eight. Drew and the others are coming over later."

I leave the mess in the sink and follow my mom as she walks through the apartment taking off her earrings, jacket, skirt. She seems to get undressed on the fly these days.

"I was hoping it'd just be the two of us tonight," I say. "Why are they coming over? Is it social?"

"No, just another strategy session about the trial. I want to make sure we're ready for anything the prosecution might throw at us. I want to make sure we don't slip up."

But my mother never slips up. Not that I can remember. I would love to move through my life as smoothly as she moves through hers.

"How was your lunch today with what's-her-name?" my mother says on her way to the bathroom.

"Morgan."

"What?"

"Her name's Morgan Hackett. It was fun." I pick up my mom's jacket and hang it in the closet. "What do you want to wear tonight? I'll get it out for you."

"Anything," she says, shouting to be heard over the running water.

I pull a rose-colored sweater out of the dresser. "Mom? Did you ever have a daydream you couldn't control?"

"A daydream I couldn't control? What are you talking about?"

I button my lip. There's no way to explain what just happened to me in the kitchen. There's just no way.

"Jamie?"

"It's nothing," I say.

"Well, it must be something or you wouldn't have brought it up."

"I just . . . I was daydreaming, sort of, and I guess that's why I lost track of how long the salmon had been under the broiler."

"Well, I wouldn't worry about it, darling. You just need to pay closer attention to what you're doing. Remember what your guidance counselor told us at the conference last month?"

"God, what a loser," I mutter.

"What?"

"Nothing." I find some white slacks in the closet and lay them out on the bed. I like the combination of rose and white. Perfect colors for a summer evening.

"He said you have enormous potential," my mother says, "but you need to work on—let's see, how did he put it—you need to work harder at staying on task."

I don't like the way this conversation is going.

"How's Sally Renfro holding up?" I ask, and my mom appears in the doorway, a towel in her hands.

"She had a hard time today," my mother says. "Not that any day is easy for her, of course. It's painful for her to see her life dissected in front of the whole world. I know there are times when she feels very much alone."

"At least she has you."

"Yes. She has me."

There's this strange little pocket of silence. The bedroom phone rings, then, and my mom picks it up. I can tell from her businesslike tone that it's one of her colleagues.

"Well, Jamie and I were just on our way out to dinner," she says. "Can't it wait till we get together later? What time is he leaving? If you think it's important, Drew . . . all right. All right, I'll meet you at the office, then."

She hangs up the phone and looks at me.

"The indispensable superlawyer," I say.

"There's a scheduling problem with the blood-spatter expert we're working with," my mother says. "We have to talk to him right away; he can't meet with us tomorrow."

"Mom, it's okay."

"I'd invite you along, but there'll be a lot of graphic details about the murder—"

"No, thanks. Sitting around and listening to gory details about blood-spatter evidence isn't exactly my idea of a fun-filled evening."

"I'll leave you some money for dinner. Don't wait up for me; I have a feeling this meeting's going to go on for hours."

*   *   *

When I call Morgan's house I get the machine, so I decide to go ahead and eat alone. It's not the greatest thing, eating alone in a restaurant. Unless you bring something to read, you think people are watching you eat, even if they're not. I hurry through my dinner because I'm so anxious to go home.

Strange, what happens next. I walk out of Pasta Mia's, and the next thing I know I'm standing at the kitchen sink in our sublet, staring at the charcoal-colored salmon in the scorched broiler pan. I'm holding my sandals, their straps looped around my index finger. I vaguely remember taking them off sometime after I left the restaurant. I think I was daydreaming about walking barefoot on the beach back home, but I'm not sure.

I go to my room and drop my sandals on the floor and fall into bed without bothering to get undressed. I think about the smoke in the kitchen before my mother came home. How I didn't see it or smell it. I think of myself outside Pasta Mia's, then suddenly home without knowing how I got here.

Sometimes when you're walking along and you stumble, there's a split second before you fall when you realize there's nothing you can do to reverse what's about to happen.

That's how I feel now. My brain has stumbled, pulled a trick on me, and one of these days I'll start falling, tumbling over and over, and I won't be able to stop.

7

IT'S BEEN OVER THREE DAYS SINCE IT
happened, since I was spirited away, hijacked to
that other dimension where I found myself back in
California with Webb. Three days, eighteen hours,
ten minutes. It's like I'm on high alert, bracing
myself for the next time I get sucked into that . . .
that daydream or whatever it was, and get spit
back out to find myself God-knows-where. I'm
hoping it doesn't show, the worry I'm carrying
about that freaky mind-slip, but Morgan's at my
side and we're walking around the city and she's
treating me like I'm perfectly normal.

"I want to show you something," she says.
We're crossing a wide metal bridge over the
Chicago River, and she stops about halfway across
and leans her arms on the railing and looks out
over the water. "My friend and I always came here
on St. Patrick's Day and watched them dye the
river green."

"Really?" I lean against the railing, too, and try
to imagine the dark water transformed into a fes-
tive green. "Did you know your friend a long time
before he died?" I ask. "Do you mind talking
about him?"

"No, he was an important part of my life; I like talking about him. Remembering him."

"Where'd you guys meet?"

"In the maternity ward," she says, laughing. "Jimmy and I were born the same week, in the same hospital, and because our mothers were friends, we were in each other's lives right from the start. Sometimes I wonder what would have happened between us if he hadn't been killed. I mean, I look back now and realize we were heading for something beyond friendship those last few months. I guess that's one of the reasons I'm not looking forward to the social scene at college. It's going to take a long time, I think, before I'm ready to get that close to another guy . . ."

"There's something so cool about starting a romance the way you and Jimmy did, as friends."

"That's how it is with you and Webb, right?"

"I don't know. I'd like it to be more than just friendship, but he wasn't very torn-up about going to Europe without me. Sometimes I think he's a little too good at playing hard-to-get."

"Give him time. My mom likes to say that my dad kept chasing her until she caught him." She points to a skyscraper across the river. "See that building? That's where my aunt's setting up her practice. C'mon; I'm dying to show you the view of the city from her office."

Morgan works for her aunt in a chrome-and-glass skyscraper that seems to disappear into the clouds. We take the elevator up to the twenty-second floor and walk past an orthodontist's office to an office at the end of the hall. There's a small brass plate on the door:

```
SUITE 2204
L. HACKETT, M.D.
```

"Here's where the magic happens," Morgan says, unlocking the door. She shows me into the waiting room. "Here's where I handle the appointment book and keep the philodendrons from drying out."

"Sounds like one of those high-stress jobs," I say.

"Hey, it's not easy keeping those magazines in neat piles, you know." She opens the door to the inner office, which is sort of small and cozy and—well, messy. There's a couch loaded with books and manila folders, a couple of chairs, and a desk that's buried under a mountain of papers.

"We're still in the process of moving in," Morgan says, shoving some boxes aside so she can walk over to the windows. "My aunt's always wanted to do this—open a downtown office. Up till now, she's had to see her private patients at the hospital."

She raises the miniblinds, and light floods the

office. The windows frame a spectacular view of the city. The skyscrapers stand like giant dominos; I picture one knocking into another knocking into another until they all fall down. I wonder if my mom's office—the office she's using while she's here in Chicago—is in one of the buildings I'm looking at. It occurs to me that I don't even know where it is.

"Hi, there."

Morgan's aunt has just breezed in and dropped her medical bag and purse onto the paper-laden desk. She has a great smile—high-voltage, almost. She could probably make a mint in our looks-obsessed culture as the face in the Lancôme ads if she ever decided to quit medicine.

"Jamie, this is my aunt, Dr. Hackett," Morgan says. "Aunt Lo, Jamie Tessman."

"Hi, Jamie. Has Morgan been giving you the grand tour around here? I keep thinking the office has possibilities, but every day we seem to accumulate more clutter."

"It's cool even with the clutter," I say, looking around. "Very . . . patient-friendly."

"Good. That's exactly what I needed to hear."

"Aunt Lo, before I forget," Morgan says, "there's some big-deal meeting at the hospital tonight." She shuffles through the papers on the desk till she finds one of those WHILE YOU WERE OUT slips. "Seven thirty in the main conference room."

"I know all about that meeting, and I'm afraid they'll just have to get along without me," Dr. Hackett says.

"They said it was important—"

"Honey, I haven't had a chance to have dinner with you all week. We're going out tonight, and that's that. Jamie, do you want to join us?"

I almost say yes. Almost. But it suddenly strikes me that dinner with a shrink probably wouldn't be a very smart thing for me to do, not with some of the peculiar things that have started happening to me lately.

"I wish I could," I say, "but I have to get back and start dinner. I like to cook, and I want to make something special for my mom tonight."

"You cook?" Morgan asks. "I'm hopeless at cooking. Maybe sometime you could show me how to boil water."

"Anytime," I say lightly. "Well, I'll call you, okay, Morgan? Bye, Dr. Hackett."

"Bye, Jamie. It was nice meeting you."

Morgan walks me to the elevators and offers to ride down with me so she can point me in the right direction for home.

"Thanks," I say, "but I'm starting to learn my way around."

"Maybe we can do something again tomorrow," she says, as I step into the elevator. "I have sort of flexible hours. One of the fringe benefits of working for a relative . . ."

There he is. I had a feeling he'd be here. I make my way down the giant rocks at Otter Cove and stand behind him and clasp my hands over his eyes so he'll have to guess who I am....

"Jamie, are you okay?" Morgan asks. She's holding the elevator door so it can't close. Her eyes are enormous. "What's wrong?"

I can feel heat wash over my face. "Nothing's wrong."

"You sort of—I don't know—you zoned out for a few seconds and it was like you couldn't see me—"

"Oh," I say, smiling. "I was up really late last night watching some lame movie on TV, and I didn't get much sleep. I guess I'm not at my sharpest today."

"As long as you're okay . . ."

"Yeah, I'm fine."

Her face relaxes, and she lets go of the elevator door. "Okay, well, give me a call later, all right?"

"I will. Bye."

She fades from view as the doors close. I'm so glad no one else is on the elevator with me. I lean my forehead against the wall and take a deep breath. There's no way to figure this out. There's just no way. It's happened again, whatever *it* is, and this time it happened in front of Morgan.

The elevator doors open, and I run across the lobby and out onto the sidewalk. The pedestrian traffic jostles me a little as I hurry to cross the street. This is what's real: the people beside me, the traffic noises, the giant skyscrapers. I'm here in Chicago and Webb's in Europe—those are the facts.

I could see him, though. I could hear the water as it rushed into the cove. I was standing behind him and . . .

I don't care what the rational part of my brain is telling me. I was with him at Otter Cove. I was *there*.

I was really there.

That is also a fact—an inexplicable fact—and it's too scary and weird to share with anyone.

8

THE BLINKING LIGHT ON THE ANSWERING
machine catches my eye as I walk into the apartment. There are three messages, all of them from my mom:

> "Jamie? I have to meet with the other lawyers in the judge's chambers after court, so I might be a little late for dinner. . . ."

> "Hi, dear . . . you'd better eat without me; Drew and I have to go over to County to talk to Sally Renfro tonight."

> "Jamie? It's me again. Don't wait up for me; this day has been absolutely impossible and I don't know when I'll be home. . . ."

It's not like I was going to tell her what happened to me earlier, or about some of the bizarre things I've started experiencing recently, so why should I care that she's going to be late? I flop down onto the couch and think of the way Morgan's aunt blew off that meeting at the hospital. "I haven't had a chance to have dinner with you all week," is the way she put it, looking at her niece. Like there was nothing in the world more important than that. It's stupid, I know, to let that bother me so much. I shouldn't compare someone else's family with my own. True, my mom's gone into overdrive with the Renfro trial, but not every case swallows her alive like this one has. Besides, I figure, at seventeen, shouldn't I be glad I don't have a mother who's constantly breathing down my neck?

It looks like I'm just going to have to accept the fact that my mom has become the Invisible Woman. I'm asleep before she comes home, and she's gone by the time I wake up the next morning. There's a note, though, taped to the bathroom mirror:

> *Lunch today? The courtroom will be packed, but I'll leave word with the bailiff if you want to come a little early and see some of the trial.*
>
> *—Mom*

So around lunchtime I toddle on down to the courthouse and go through the metal detector, pushing through the halls that are chock full of reporters and media people, their minicams balanced on their shoulders as they wait for court to adjourn. A few words to the bailiff, then, and I'm allowed to slip into the courtroom and stand in the back.

The prosecutor's on his feet, questioning some dull-looking guy on the witness stand. Mom's watching it all like a hawk, leaning over once in a while to whisper something to Sally Renfro.

"Objection," Mom says suddenly. "Prejudicial."

And from the judge: "Sustained. Rephrase."

I love seeing Mom in action. I'm totally in awe of her chameleonlike ability in court to change personalities at a moment's notice: to go from caring, maternal type to zero-tolerance hit man; whatever it takes to unnerve a witness or one of the prosecuting attorneys.

"Objection!" Mom says. "Lack of foundation, Your Honor. And again, the prosecutor has misstated the evidence."

"Sustained. Let's move on, Mr. Jefferies."

Mom's getting under the prosecutor's skin—I can see it. He's a young guy, probably hoping he'll make a name for himself with this case. *Just give it up, buddy,* I think. *You don't know who you're dealing with here.*

When court breaks for lunch and most everyone has filed out, I wander up to the defense table and start helping my mom pack some of her wayward papers into her briefcase.

"Allow me to introduce myself," I say. "I'm your daughter. Remember me?"

"Vaguely," she says, smiling. "Have I been too negligent? You aren't into any illegal activities I should know about, are you?"

"Don't worry. I know a terrific lawyer, even if she *is* a bit expensive."

"I could always give you a family discount." She closes her briefcase. "Let's leave by the side door and avoid the crowd."

Lunch is a semipetrified sandwich from a machine near the jury commissioner's office.

"What ambiance," I say, as Mom shows me a nice hard bench where we can eat.

"We'd be mobbed in the cafeteria."

"That's what you get for being a media darling." I tuck my legs up under me and peel the cellophane off my sandwich. We suddenly seem to be at a loss for words. Sometimes I think my mom and I are like a couple of strangers who struggle to make conversation.

I take a bite of my sandwich. Should I tell her? Should I tell her I'm afraid something really freaky is going on with me? I tried to do it the other day, sort of. It didn't work out too well.

"What did you do today?" my mom asks. "Anything fun?"

"Not yet. I'll call Morgan this afternoon and see if she wants to get together later."

"You'll have to bring her over to the apartment sometime," she says. "I'd like to meet her."

"You're kidding, right? You're never home."

"Okay, I deserved that. I know this week has been a little crazy, darling, but I'm hoping things will settle down as the trial goes on."

"Looks like you've got the Renfro girl all

decked out as Suzy Sorority," I say. "Blue sweater, matching skirt, and wow—that retro ponytail."

"That's the idea. Everybody's all-American college girl."

"I really feel sorry for that prosecutor. It's probably his first big case, and he has *you* to deal with."

"I was a prosecutor for too many years; I know all the tricks."

I search through my backpack till I find a clipping from the morning paper: a picture of Mom on the courthouse steps, the headline in bold type:

TESSMAN DELIVERS BLOW TO PROSECUTION

"Did you see this?" I ask, and Mom takes the clipping from me and reads it. "You were on the morning news, too," I tell her. "The publicity on this trial is unbelievable."

"I know. It reminds me of the Carson White trial," she says. "Do you remember it? No. Maybe not. You were only nine at the time."

"No, I remember—he was on trial for molesting a child, right? You prosecuted him."

My mother shudders. "That was such a scary time. I never told you this because you were so young, but as soon as we went to trial I started getting some frightening mail. Threats, actually."

"Threats? What kinds of threats? From the defendant, you mean?"

"We never knew. From the defendant, or from someone who knew him, or maybe from some psycho who'd read about me in the paper. The police couldn't trace the letters back to anyone, so they kept an eye on me until the trial was over. On you, too. An officer always watched to make sure you got to and from school safely."

"You mean I was *tailed*?" I can't help it: I burst out laughing. "Cool! I bet I was the only nine-year-old with a bodyguard!"

My mom takes a bite of her sandwich. "That trial was so disturbing. There was so much outrage against Carson White that someone went after his family one night—shot and killed his brother."

"Mom, please! I'm trying to eat!"

She smiles a bit sheepishly. "Sorry."

"If we could get off the subject of murder and onto something much more vital—like food—how about parting with some of your hard-earned cash? I want to do a little shopping for dinner."

"How much do you need?"

"Fifty?"

"What are we having for dinner? Caviar?"

"I'm going to cook ahead for next week," I say. "Then whenever my disappearing mother actually shows up, I can just take something out of the freezer and zap it in the microwave. Clever, right?"

"Extremely clever." She counts out some crisp bills and hands them to me. "I should be home early tonight, unless something unforeseen happens."

Clack, clack, clack: high heels echoing on the highly polished floor. I recognize the woman: one of the other lawyers seated at the defense table.

"Excuse me, Min, there're some things I have to go over with you before the afternoon session."

"I'll be right there," Mom says. She throws me an "I'm sorry" look. "See you at dinner?"

"Six o'clock. Chicken paella. Don't be late."

"Bye." She gathers up her briefcase and purse and starts off down the hall.

"Mom?"

She turns around and looks at me.

"Whatever happened to Carson White?" I ask. "I mean, I know you got him convicted of child molesting—"

"He was killed in prison," my mother says. "Knifed to death. Not much of a loss, if you ask me." She shrugs, then heads back down the hall.

9

"I SAW YOUR MOM ON THE NEWS THIS morning," Morgan says. We're seated at a sidewalk café. It's a warm, windy, blue-sky kind of day, the lunch looks wonderful, but I can't enjoy anything at the moment. I'm too busy trying to stay focused on the here and now. I have the uneasy sensation that something is tugging at me, pulling at me, trying to take me away somewhere.

"I guess you're pretty used to it, though," Morgan says.

"Used to what?"

"Seeing your mom on the news all the time."

"Oh. Well, it's not all the time. It's just when she's involved in a well-known case like the Renfro trial." I rub my eyes. I'm having a hard time staying awake. "She worked on a trial like this when I was nine. There was a lot of publicity, and—"

"This is probably none of my business," Morgan says, and I brace myself for something intrusive, because nobody starts a sentence that way unless it's followed by something really obnoxious, "but are you okay? You don't look too good."

Not as bad as I was worried about; she's just concerned.

"I'm just sort of tired," I say. "My mom didn't get home till after two in the morning, and I waited up for her."

"I guess working on the trial takes up a lot of her time, huh?"

"Yeah, after court adjourns for the day she and the other lawyers get together and . . ."

"Remember all those nights your mom worked late, Jamie?" Webb asks. "You'd call me and we'd make a date to meet here on the beach."

"The hardest part was making sure I got home before my mom did. I had a couple of close calls, but she never caught me; she never knew I'd sneaked away. . . ."

"Jamie?" Morgan's saying, shaking me hard. "Jamie! Are you okay?"

I'm horrified to see that Morgan's moved from across the table and is standing right next to me. A waiter hurries over and says, "Is there a problem? Should I call someone?"

"No, I . . ." Morgan looks at me. "Are you okay?"

I can't talk, so I just nod. The waiter slowly walks away, and Morgan drops some cash on the table. "Look, maybe we should go home. . . ."

I slide out of the booth. I want to run, but I don't want to draw any more attention to myself, so I settle for a brisk stride. *It's happened again*, I think. *It's happened* again.

"Jamie, wait!" Morgan hurries to catch up with me. "What happened back there? Are you okay? Maybe we should call your mom."

I stop walking and turn to her. "Just tell me," I say. "Tell me what I did."

"You sort of—I don't know—it was like you were asleep, sort of, only your eyes were open. You seemed so far away. Jamie, are you sick? I mean, what's wrong?"

"I can't explain what I don't understand." I'm shaking, that's how rattled I am. "Morgan, look, you can't tell anyone about this; I'd die if my mom found out."

"Jamie, you have to tell her—"

"No! I put my mom through hell this spring. She's finally at a point where she's stopped monitoring my every move, and I'm not going to give her anything new to worry about."

"But this could be serious," she says. "What if it happens when you're crossing the street or . . ." I can see she's figured something out; she's put two and two together. "This is why you had that bike accident. . . ."

My throat's dry. My voice comes out in a monotone: "I had a daydream about him that was so vivid—so *real*. I came out of it right before I ran my bike into a parked car. The next thing I knew, a couple of paramedics were shoving me into an ambulance. God, this is so embarrassing." I start walking again. She's right beside me.

"Jamie, look, it's okay. You don't have to worry about what I think."

"It never happened before we came here to Chicago. Never. It's like I get pulled into another world, and I can't help it. When it happens, Webb and I are together again, walking on the beach or sitting next to each other at the park where we first met." I glance at her. "You must think I'm really messed up."

"No, I told you: I've had problems too."

"Not like mine."

"No, I was crazy in my own unique way."

"Morgan, promise you won't tell anyone about this."

"Who would I tell?"

"Just promise."

"Okay," she says. "Okay. I promise."

She walks me back to the apartment building, comes upstairs, makes me a cup of tea.

"How is it?" she asks.

"You left the tea bag in too long."

Her lips curl into a smile. "I warned you that I couldn't even boil water, remember?"

I take another sip of tea: It's bitter, but I don't care. I'm just glad she's here; glad that I'm not alone.

Morgan sits cross-legged on the floor and tells me some stuff about herself: how she slept in her friend's jacket every night for months after his death. She's giving me a little piece of herself, sort of—letting me see I'm not the only one who's had a brush with nuttiness.

I sit back and listen to her. I can feel myself start to quiet down inside. I don't mind that she saw me flip out. I was worried she'd think I was twisted, but she didn't.

She's seen me at my worst and likes me anyway. Incredible.

10

AT FIRST I THINK IT'S AN ANIMAL making those rustling sounds in the bushes. A raccoon, maybe, or a deer. There's plenty of moonlight tonight, but I can't be sure of what I'm looking at. The gnarled scrub oaks throw contorted shadows over the edge of the baseball field and play tricks on my eyes. I hear the sound of dry leaves crunching underfoot, then I hear his words:

"Jamie? I'm not going to hurt you. . . ."

I sit bolt upright in bed, gasping for air. It's been a long time since I've had any kind of nightmare, and years since I've had this one. I had forgotten these terrifying dream images—images of being helpless and pursued. When I was little and had nightmares, my mom would sit with me until the world became real to me again.

I swing my legs over the edge of the bed and hurry out into the hall and peek inside my mother's room. I think about what I might say to her when I wake her up:

"Mom, I had a bad dream. . . ."

"Mom, I'm afraid to go back to sleep. . . ."

"Mom, I'm so scared. . . ."

She sleeps soundly, her hand open and relaxed against the pillow. I stand there a moment watching her sleep, listening to her breathe, listening to the clock ticking, ticking . . . the clock's luminescent numbers show that it's four thirty. I start to touch her shoulder, but I just can't bring myself to wake her, to rob her of the hour and a half of sleep she has left before the alarm rings at six. I don't want her walking into the morning session of court feeling like a zombie.

I go back to my room and pull the blanket off my bed. Once I have it wrapped around me, I sit in the chair by the window and stare at some twinkling lights off in the distance somewhere. The images of the dream start to tumble together in wild kaleidoscopic patterns: the gnarled scrub oaks, the baseball field, the flash of something moving in the bushes. I can practically hear that voice from my dream, a voice soothing and low, a voice that's gentle, but doesn't tell the truth:

"I'm not going to hurt you, Jamie. . . ."

It isn't until dawn that I start to feel better. From the window I watch as the city begins to wake up, then I hear my mom's alarm go off, and I stumble into the kitchen to start the coffee.

That terrifying dream seems as far away as a distant star now, and has no more power to harm me than a backyard firefly, winking to get my attention.

11

I'M ON MY WAY HOME FROM THE GROCERY store the next day when I see him—at least, I *think* it's him, it *could* be him, up ahead, in a sea of pedestrians hurrying home after work. It's possible that he just woke up one morning and decided he'd seen enough of Europe. It'd be just like him to hop on a plane to Chicago and show up unannounced so he could surprise me. Maybe he saw an article about my mom in the paper and tracked down our address by contacting the law firm she's working with here in the city. All these possibilities are spinning in my head as I hurry to get a better look at him. He has a newspaper tucked under one arm and he carries a duffel bag, like the kind he takes to the gym. I wonder where he's staying. How long he'll be here. He's too far away to hear me if I yell his name, but I say it under my breath, sort of like a prayer: "Webb, slow down, just slow down so I can catch up with you. . . ." And he *does* slow down. He slows down when he gets to the middle of the block. He stops in front of our apartment building. He slings the duffel bag over his shoulder and waits.

"Jamie!" Not Webb, but from behind me, my

mom's voice: "I've been calling you; didn't you hear me?"

"No . . ."

She takes one of the grocery bags from me. "What's wrong? You look so pale."

"Nothing's wrong; I'm just sort of surprised to see you. How come you're home so early?" As we approach our building, I see that he's gone. I wonder why he left. Or maybe I'm wrong: Maybe it wasn't Webb at all. A scarier explanation looms: Maybe my mind is shattering, and there wasn't *anyone* there.

"The judge had an appointment, so we adjourned at four," my mother says. "I was thinking maybe we could go out someplace nice for dinner—"

"No, I want to make something," I say. "Tortellini Alfredo with roasted peppers, okay?"

"Wonderful. You're just like your dad. He was a great cook. Do you remember that? Do you remember anything at all about your dad? You were so little when he died."

"I remember *some* things about him," I say. "He used to read to me, didn't he? Poetry, I think. And *Alice in Wonderland*."

"He loved reading to you, playing with you, taking you to the park, the wharf, Otter Cove. . . ."

"I wish I remembered more about him."

"So do I," my mom says wistfully.

❋   ❋   ❋

I know my mother meant it when she said we'd have dinner together. And we do eat together. Technically, anyway. For most of the meal, though, she's on the phone, hashing over various problems with her lawyer pals.

"Drew, you and I both know someone in the DA's office has been talking to the media," she says. "Did you see this morning's *Sun-Times*? And on WBBM this morning, too—oh, hold on a second, Drew; I have another call. . . ."

And on and on . . .

"It was wonderful, darling, thank you," my mother says, her hand over the mouthpiece of the phone as I take her plate to the kitchen. She didn't eat very much. I don't take it personally—I know my mom likes my cooking—but everything takes a backseat when she's wrapped up in a trial, even something as necessary as dinner. I cover her plate and put it on the stove to keep it warm; she might want it later.

"I think I'll go across the street to Pasta Mia's for a gelato," I say, and she nods and continues her phone conversation:

"We'll just have to go over it during the afternoon recess tomorrow," she says. "No, I really don't have any other free time. . . ."

It's hot out on the street. Humid. Pasta Mia's has already closed, but I didn't really want a gelato, anyway. I'm here to take another look around. Just one more look.

I don't see him. I wonder if I ever did. Maybe I saw someone who resembled Webb from a distance, and I made a mistake, that's all. Anyone can make a mistake.

So he's not here. He never was. He's probably still backpacking through Europe, having the time of his life. God only knows how many girls he's meeting.

I think about our last afternoon together, when we sat on the giant rocks in Otter Cove, his hands gently gathering my hair into a ponytail. I'd give anything if I could go back in time and live that afternoon all over again. If I close my eyes, if I try hard enough, I can almost believe I'm there. . . .

Webb wraps his arms around me, and I settle back against him. "Here comes the show," he says, and we laugh as the otters glide into the cove and begin chasing each other around the rocks.

There is nowhere else on earth I would rather be than right here, here with Webb at my side.

12

MY MOM WORKS LATE THE NEXT NIGHT, SO I
ask Morgan to come over for dinner. I've started
to dread being alone. Too many peculiar things
seem to happen to me when I'm alone. Morgan's
good company: she compliments me on the
Szechwan chicken and doesn't let the silence drag
on just because I'm not in a talking mood.

My big contribution to the conversation is
what triggers the argument. I hadn't even
planned on bringing it up, but it must have been
lurking in the back of my head because I just
blurt it out:

"What was I like the other day when I zoned
out?" I ask. "I must have done something really
weird, right? I mean, the waiter came over, and
people were staring—"

"No, you didn't do anything weird." We've finished dinner and she's helping me scrape the
plates and load them into the dishwasher. "I guess
I'm the one who drew attention to you because I
was shouting at you, trying to get you to wake up
or—well, trying to get your attention."

"I thought I saw Webb here in the city yesterday." I don't want to sound all freaky and worried,

but I can't help it. Morgan leans back against the kitchen counter and waits for me to go on. "I still don't know if it was someone who looked like him, or if I was just dreaming."

"Jamie," Morgan says, "you have to tell your mom."

All sorts of internal alarms start going off. "I can't."

"You have to. You have to tell her about this zoning-out thing—"

"God, I'm sorry I even brought it up." I slam the dishwasher door shut. I hope she gets the message. "I got a little mixed-up yesterday, that's all. So what. Big deal."

She gives me a "You've got to be kidding" look. We both know I'm full of it. We both know I'm more than a little mixed-up.

"Jamie, look, maybe it'd be a good idea if you saw someone. You know. A doctor."

"What—like your aunt, you mean? No thanks. I'm not crazy."

"I didn't say you were crazy. You could talk it over with your mom, and if you'd like, I could—"

"I didn't ask for any advice."

There's a terrible icy silence between us.

The front door opens and shuts.

"Jamie?" my mom calls. "I left a couple of my files here, and—oh," she says, surprised, but smiling when she sees Morgan. "Hi. You must be Morgan, right?"

"Hi, Mrs. Tessman. I feel like I already know you, in a way, because I've seen you on the news so much. I don't know how you handle all those reporters shouting questions at you day after day—"

"It's not easy," she says in a mock serious tone, "but I do it because I have to. I'm Min Tessman: defender of truth, justice, and the American way."

Morgan and I both laugh, and I can feel some of the iciness between us melt just a bit.

"Szechwan chicken," my mom says, taking a little piece of chicken from the skillet. "Hmm . . . wonderful. Jamie's always been a great chef, even when she was little. She used to look so cute with her apron touching the tops of her shoes—"

"Groan. Mom, you didn't come home just to tell embarrassing childhood stories about me, did you?"

"No, I forgot some of my files . . . ah, there they are." She searches through a stack of folders piled on the kitchen counter. "Don't wait up for me, Jamie; I'm afraid this meeting will last till all hours." She tucks the folders into her briefcase. "Well," she says, "see you later, darling. You two have a fun evening, all right?"

As soon as we're alone, Morgan turns to me and says, "Look, I'm sorry. I shouldn't have given you advice when you weren't asking for any. It's none of my business."

I shrug. "It's okay."

"So am I forgiven?"

"For what? Butting into my life, you mean?"

"Yeah. I don't usually do things like that. I guess I was just—"

"You were just worried about me. I know. It's nice, in a way, to have a friend who's so concerned about me that she tells me how to live my life. Even if she *is* totally wrong."

That gets a smile out of her. "I won't butt into your life again," she says. "I promise. You know what I'd like to do? Make it up to you by showing you some of Chicago's night-life. Do you have a newspaper? We can see what's going on around town."

"I think there's a *Tribune* around here somewhere."

The newspaper's folded neatly on the coffee table, but just as I'm reaching for it, I notice one of my mother's legal files on the floor. "I hope my mom didn't need this for her meeting. . . ." When I pick up the folder, a glossy photograph slides out of it and lands at my feet.

"Is that a picture of what I *think* it is?" Morgan asks.

The photograph, labeled Renfro Crime Scene, shows a close-up of a man lying on a rug. His eyes are open and lifeless, his skin gray. Dark red blood fans around his head like some sort of obscene halo. I'm so horrified at first that I'm frozen; then I snatch the picture up and shove it back into the folder.

"God, why can't she be a tax attorney," I say,

"or a divorce lawyer? Why does she have be a criminal defense attorney? It was bad enough back when she was a prosecutor—"

"I can't stand the sight of blood either," Morgan says. "And something about that picture is just so . . . so . . ."

"Creepy," I say.

"Yeah. Creepy."

I drop the folder on the table. My hands are shaking badly. "Let's get out of here, okay, Morgan? I'm ready to do something fun."

"Yeah, so am I," she says, looking through the newspaper. "I think there's a new club opening up just a couple blocks from here. Do you like jazz?"

"Anything's fine," I say, heading for my bedroom. "I'll be right back; I want to get my backpack."

It's not just the backpack I need. I need to sit down on the bed and be quiet a minute. I need to stop shaking. I need to forget that horrendous photograph. I need . . .

Webb stands on the bike trail down by the bay. It's almost dusk now, and the chilly fog hazes up a purple-pink sunset.

"Cold, Jamie!" He shouts to me. "You picked a hell of a night to come back for a visit. Starting to rain, too."

"Wow, what a greeting," I shout back, and he laughs and holds out his hand. I love the

way our hands fit together—like they were
made for each other. A perfect match.

"Jamie?" Morgan says. "What's wrong? Are you okay? *Jamie?*"

I can barely hear her; she's too far away. I'm guessing she's just walked into my room and discovered I've disappeared, pulled a vanishing act. She must be plenty scared, but what can I do about it from here?

I turn away from the faint sound of her voice and follow Webb down to the water.

✳ **PART TWO** ✳

PART TWO

13

So what is it? Webb asks. What s wrong?

How d you know?

I can always tell when something s bothering you. He leads me off the bike trail, and we step up onto some rocks overlooking the bay.

Some weird things have started happening to me, I say. Things I don t understand. Things I can t explain.

Like what?

Like thinking I saw you in the city when you weren t there . . . or daydreaming about you so much the real world vanishes . . . or having that nightmare I haven t had since I was little, but is still so frightening I wake up in the middle of the night with my heart pounding . . .

From far away, I hear a woman's voice: "I want a neurologist to take a look at her. Who's on tonight?"

And another voice: "Scovell's on. Brooks, too, I think."

"Give Dr. Scovell a call, please, and tell him I need a consult here in the ER."

"Right away . . ."

And another voice: "Dr. Hackett, Jamie's tox screen came back negative."

"Good. Have you been able to reach her mother?"

"Still trying . . ."

And another voice: "Dr. Hackett? Your niece wants to know if she can come in—"

"No. Not yet."

Webb looks at me with a sort of helpless understanding. Jamie, things are a little rough for you right now, but everything will be all right . . . everything will be fine.

> *Do you really think so?*
> *I wouldn t say it if I didn t believe it.*

Suddenly my foot slips on the wet rocks, and the next thing I know I m in the cold water of the bay. It s not so deep right here, but the waves pull me back, back, back, and now I m sinking, breathing foamy water. I m going to drown, I think, drown because there s nothing underfoot and nothing to hang on to. Nothing to save me. Then I feel a hand grasp mine.

> *A perfect match, our hands.*

He pulls me up to the surface and back to the beach where it s safe.

> *Are you all right? he asks.*
> *Are you?*
> *His laugh is shaky: No . . .*

You saved my life.
It's not the first time.
No, I say. It's not the first time.

"Jamie? You almost came back once; don't drift away from me again. Open your eyes."

I open my eyes, and it hits me instantly: I'm in the emergency room, in the same type of curtained-off cubicle they put me in the night I had the bike accident. I recognize the person standing next to the bed—Morgan's aunt. I can't figure out why she's here, though, not at first, not until I notice the stethoscope draped around her neck. My adrenaline starts pumping. I get it now: She's not here as my friend's aunt. She's here because she's a doctor, and there's something very wrong with me.

"It's all right," the doctor says. She's speaking in a reassuring tone that doesn't make me feel any better. "You know who I am, don't you?"

"Dr. Hackett."

"Yes. Jamie, there was a problem earlier. Do you remember any of it?"

"Did Morgan . . ." I begin. "Did I do something that made her call you?"

"You had some sort of episode tonight while you were with her," the doctor says. "When you couldn't snap out of it, she called me, and we got you here to the hospital."

It all comes flooding back to me now: the dinner with Morgan, seeing that creepy photograph, then *zap*—that tremendous free-fall into the Twilight Zone.

They've got me hooked up to a monitor that has a bunch of spiky lines dancing across it. I have the uneasy feeling that if the lines on that screen collapse, so will I.

"That's your heart," the doctor says, glancing at the monitor. "I know all this equipment's pretty intimidating; the ER doctor and I are just trying to find out what caused the blackout you had."

"But I'm okay, right? I don't have to stay here, do I?"

"We're going to keep you here overnight," she says. "I have a neurologist coming in to take a look at you, and he'll want to run a few tests—"

"Tests? I don't need any tests. I daydream sometimes. Maybe Morgan told you. I daydream a little. That doesn't mean I'm sick, does it?"

"Nope." She reaches for this flashlight-type thing attached to the wall with a curly cord. "Look at me," she says, and suddenly the light flares in my eyes. "And over my shoulder . . . are you under a doctor's care right now for any medical problems?"

"No."

"How often does it happen? How often do you drift away like you did earlier?"

"I don't know. Just . . . once in a while, I guess."

"Who's Webb?"

I pull away from her. "How do you know about Webb? Did Morgan . . . did she—"

"No, you did," the doctor says, clicking off the

light. "You've been talking to him ever since the paramedics brought you in."

Talking to him? I broadcast that entire day-dream for the whole world to hear? "He's a friend of mine," I say, struggling to keep my voice calm. "It's been hard for me, sort of, since we've been apart this summer."

A nurse sticks her head inside the curtain: "Dr. Hackett? We finally reached Jamie's mother; she's on the way."

"Thank you."

I prop myself up on one elbow. "What are you going to tell my mom?" I ask the doctor. "She's the lead attorney on the Renfro trial—maybe you knew that—and she's under a lot of pressure. I don't want to worry her."

"What don't you want me to tell her?"

I drop my head back against the pillow. "I don't know. There isn't anything, I guess."

The doctor reaches up and adjusts one of her ear-rings: a small, square-cut emerald. "Everything you've talked about in here is private. I won't repeat it to anyone."

"Everything? Even when I was . . ." I look at her. "If my mom—God, my friend's in Europe right now—if my mom finds out I was talking to him like he was in the room or something—"

"Daydreams are also kept confidential," she says, smiling a little. "Okay?"

"Yeah. Okay."

"Morgan keeps asking to see you. Is it all right if I send her in?"

"I'd like that."

She pulls the curtains open and motions Morgan inside. I'm glad when the doctor takes her chart out to the nurses' station; glad it's just Morgan and me.

"Hi," she says. She walks over to the bed slowly and grips the guardrail like she's all tense. "Are you okay?"

"A lot better than you are, I think."

"I was so worried about you."

"You broke your promise."

"About butting into your life, yeah. Sorry about that."

"No, I'm glad you . . . I didn't want you to see me like that again, though . . . like . . ." Without warning, tears sting my eyes. "I never know when it's going to happen," I whisper. "I never *know.*"

"Jamie, it's okay."

"I can't explain any of it."

"You don't have to."

"Will you stay with me till my mom gets here?"

She nods and pulls up a stool and sits next to the bed. We don't do any more talking. Morgan seems to take her cue from me, she's intuitive in that way, I can see, and seems to know how tired am. I close my eyes and think about what's ahead: I still have my mom to deal with and that neurologist person and those tests. Not to mention Dr. Hackett. I get the feeling she can see right into me. It's hard to fool a person like that. If I can just stay connected to reality when I'm around her, then maybe she'll decide I'm okay and let me go home tomorrow.

All I have to do is hold things together while I'm talking to her.

I can do that. I know I can.

14

MY MOM STANDS IN THE DOORWAY, watching for the doctor. She looks like hell—she spent the entire night here, sleeping in the chair next to my bed.

"Mom, you only have forty-five minutes to get to court, you know."

"I'm not going anywhere until we talk to the doctor."

"Well, who knows when she'll get here? Why don't you go ahead, and I'll call you after I see her?"

"That'd be a lovely thing for a mother to do, now, wouldn't it? Trot off to work while her only daughter is lying helpless in a hospital room in a strange city."

"Do I look helpless?"

"I think the last time you were helpless you were wearing diapers."

"What a picture. Please don't mention it to any future boyfriends I may have."

She's dead tired, but she smiles anyway. "I'll try to remember."

A quiet knock on the open door, and here's the doctor. She looks a lot different than she did last night: Last night she was in casual clothes; today it's all business, right down to the white coat and hospital ID tag.

"Morning," she says. "How do you feel? Ready to go home?"

"Can I?"

She nods. "I want to talk to you and your mom first, though." She sits on the bed and clasps her hands around one knee. "You know, Dr. Scovell and I have gone over the lab work and the scan you had, Jamie, and everything seems to be normal—"

"Oh," my mom says, the worry vanishing from her face, "I can't tell you how relieved I am. I was so concerned."

"—but," the doctor adds, "I still don't know why Jamie drifted away from us last night, or why it took her so long to come back."

"What exactly happened when she drifted away?" my mom asks. "You didn't go into too much detail last night."

The doctor looks at me, and I hold my breath. She said it was private, what I'd talked about in the emergency room—now we'll see if she meant it.

"The episode Jamie had last night was a sort of waking dream," the doctor says. "It was very hard for her to snap back to reality."

I relax a little; too soon, as it turns out.

My mother frowns. "But why did it happen? Why would she slip into this . . . this dream state?"

"That's what we have to find out."

"So it's serious, then," my mother says. "You're talking about . . . about . . ."

The doctor's going to say something I won't like. I just know it. I can tell from the way she's looking at me.

"Jamie needs psychiatric help."

"No!" My voice is so loud it bounces off the walls of the room. "I don't need that kind of help." I look at my mother. "Mom, *please* . . ."

My mother reaches over and puts her hand on mine. "Let's just listen to what she has to say."

"Jamie," the doctor says quietly, "what happened last night was a warning. A warning that something's wrong."

I'm waiting for my mom to tell the doctor off. She'll stick up for me. She'll defend me, even though I guess I haven't been accused of anything. But my mom surprises me: "Dr. Hackett, I've been worried about Jamie for the past few months. She had a lot of problems in school this spring and—"

"*Everyone* had problems there." I pull away from her hand. "It was like a giant nursery school. You checked your brain at the door."

"I'm talking about outpatient treatment," the doctor says. "In my downtown office, Jamie. Or, if you'd like, I can refer you to another psychiatrist."

"I'm not going to you or anyone else. The whole idea is stupid."

I sound incredibly rude. I don't care. My mother does.

"*Jamie!*"

"She doesn't *know* me. She doesn't know anything *about* me."

It's hard to read the doctor's expression: tolerant, sort of; maybe a little amused, too. She pulls a prescription pad out of her coat pocket and jots something down on it.

"I'll give you my number," she says, "and you can decide whether or not you want to call me."

The doctor tears off the top sheet of paper and hands it to me. Her phone number's scrawled across it. It's all I can do not to rip it up and throw the pieces at her.

"We'll call and make an appointment," my mother says.

Like hell, I think.

My mother walks Dr. Hackett to the door. Mom looks the way she does in court—cool and calm—exactly the opposite of what I know she's feeling inside.

"I'll go sign your release forms," the doctor says, "and you can leave anytime."

"Thank you," my mom answers, like the doctor's doing us a big favor by stopping by to ruin my life.

As soon as the doctor's gone, I crumple up her phone number and toss it across the room, where it bounces off the edge of a wastebasket. "God, these shrinks want to turn everything into some deep dark psychological problem."

My mother scoops up the piece of paper and smoothes it out.

"Mom, you think I need a *psychiatrist*? Please."

"I think," my mom says, "that the doctor's right. I think there's a problem, and I think I'm worried about it."

"You're worried about the wrong things. You should be worrying about the way you look."

"What's wrong with the way I look?"

"Nothing, if you're doing an impression of an anemic ghost. You better put some blush on."

She tucks the doctor's phone number into her purse. "What a nag."

"That's what I'm here for."

I grab my clothes and hurry into the bathroom. In less than two minutes I've peeled off my hospital attire and I'm into my jeans and sweatshirt. When I come out Mom's got her face pinked-up, and a nurse is waiting with a wheelchair.

"You have to ride down," Mom says. "Regulations, you know."

"Whatever." I plop down into the chair. I'm just so glad to be getting out of here.

Webb sneaks up behind me and grabs me around the waist; then he laughs and takes off into the fog.

Jamie! he shouts. Race you to Cannery Row!

Hey, who said you could give yourself a head start?

Aw, poor baby!

I start after him.   Okay, Webb! Fine! We
see how funny you think it is once I get my
hands on you!

He s so far ahead of me I can barely see
him, but I m not worried. Sooner or later I ll
catch up with him; I always do. It s just a ques-
tion of time.

15

MY MOTHER DROPS A BOMB ON ME THE day after I'm released from the hospital. I mean, I've hardly had a chance to catch my breath since I've been home, and this morning, right before she leaves for court, she comes into the bathroom while I'm brushing my teeth and says: "I made an appointment for you with Dr. Hackett."

"You *what*?" I spit out a mouthful of toothpaste. "Mom, I don't need a psychiatrist!"

"Tomorrow at two o'clock." She turns and walks out, just like that. I wipe my mouth on the back of my hand and run after her.

"Tomorrow! Why didn't you *tell* me?"

"I'm telling you now."

"You didn't even ask me!"

"I'm aware of that."

"I'm not going!"

She raises an eyebrow, then starts loading papers into her briefcase. "We've finally met someone who seems to have uncovered a problem that exists; who seems to have some insight—"

"The *doctor*? You're talking about the *doctor*? I don't think she's so insightful! I don't think she knows *anything*!"

"I've checked around. She has an excellent reputation."

"I don't care! I'm not going to see her!"

"Yes, you are." She snaps the latches shut on her briefcase. "Tomorrow at two. End of discussion."

"Mom, I've never heard you *talk* like this! You sound so . . . so cold!"

She comes over and puts her arms around me. "We both know there's something wrong. Something serious. I want you to get some help, darling."

Now I'm almost crying. "Why don't you just say it? You think I'm crazy."

"No. Not crazy. Just very confused about something." She takes my hands in hers. "Tomorrow at two. Promise me."

She looks so worried it scares me.

"Okay," I say, almost in a whisper. "Okay, I promise."

He s waiting in the park tonight; the park where we first met.

Did you hear? I ask.

Your moms making you see a shrink. Yeah. I heard.

Everything s falling apart, I say. Do you remember how scared I was the night we met? That s how I feel now. That s how I feel about seeing this doctor.

I ll never forget that night, Webb says. There you were, all alone on the baseball field, crying because it was getting dark. I wanted to protect you that night, Jamie. I still do.

I m not nine years old anymore, Webb. You can t protect me from everything.

He doesn t try to argue; he just wraps his arms around me. Something about being locked into that bear hug makes me feel better; better than I have in days.

It was easier to protect you back when you were a kid, Webb says quietly. Back when you were nine, when the only thing you were afraid of was the dark.

16

"I'M SEEING YOUR AUNT TOMORROW AT
two," I tell Morgan on the phone that night. "Did
you know?"

"Yeah, I saw your name in the appointment
book," she says. "I'm guessing you're majorly pet-
rified, right?"

"That's putting it mildly." I'm in my room because
my mom and her lawyer friends have taken over the
living room and are discussing every detail of the trial
as well as Sally Renfro's fragile state of mind. I don't
want to hear any of it; I have enough problems of my
own.

"So what happens when I walk in there tomorrow?" I ask. "Does she throw a bunch of inkblots
at me or hypnotize me or something?"

"I think it's mostly just talking."

"Just talking?" I bite my thumbnail. "I'm not
even sure I can handle talking at this point. I basically want to get into bed and pull the blanket
over my head and hibernate."

"Yeah, I know what that's like. Jamie, look, it's
going to be fine. I promise."

"You *promise*? You're sort of famous for breaking promises, remember?" I say, and she laughs.

"Not this one."

"It must have been really bad for you when I flipped out," I say.

"Yeah, I was worried."

I lace my fingers through the phone cord. "I'm really, really scared, Morgan."

"I know," she says. "Look, not that it helps a whole lot, but I'm working tomorrow afternoon, so I'll be there when you come in."

"It helps," I say. The discussion about the Renfro trial is growing heated and louder, so I kick my door shut. "Moral support isn't that easy to come by, so yeah, it helps a lot, knowing you'll be there."

I am sick the next morning. Literally. Like not being able to keep breakfast down. I figure this should earn me a little mom-sympathy. I'm wrong.

"It's just nerves," my mom says as she hustles to get ready for court. "It's only natural to be a little apprehensive before your first visit to a psychiatrist—"

"*Visit?* You make it sound like I'm going to tea or something."

"You'll feel much better tonight, I'm sure."

"Mom, I'm *sick*."

She slides into her jacket. "Jamie, I don't have time for this. You're not sick."

"I'm not sick, so you're forcing me to go to a doctor," I say. "How . . . how . . ."

"Ironic?" my mother asks. She picks up her briefcase. "Call me after your appointment. We usually adjourn for the afternoon recess about three, but if I'm still in court, I want you to leave a message on my voice mail and tell me how it went." She gives me a hug; then she's out the door.

Of course I could skip the appointment, but part of me doesn't want to. I'm not sure why, exactly. Morgan's one reason, I guess: I dragged her into my problems, and now the least I can do is show her I intend to do something about them.

At two o'clock I walk into the waiting room of L. Hackett, M.D. It looked a lot friendlier the last time I saw it, back when I was just a sightseer; before I was a patient. Morgan's waiting for me, a can of Diet Coke in one hand, a bottle of juice in the other.

"And I just started some coffee, if you'd rather have that," she says.

"Thanks, but I don't really feel like anything right now. Except leaving, of course." I glance at the door to the inner office. "Do I just knock or go in or what?"

"She's not back from the hospital yet," Morgan says. "Would you like to sit down?"

"I think I'll just pace, if you don't mind."

"Well, sure. Go ahead. Pace."

The waiting room is small, but I pace anyway. Morgan sits on her desk and watches me. "I had a guidance counselor this spring who kept trying to analyze me," I say. "He'd haul me into his office and ask if I had any self-esteem issues. God, what a jerk."

"It won't be like that with my aunt," Morgan says. "She's not one of those—I don't know—pseudo-intellectual types. She's very easy to talk to."

I'm thinking I might just bolt, despite my brave intentions when I walked in here, but it's too late: The doctor has just breezed in.

"Jamie, I'm sorry I'm late," she says. "I got stuck in a meeting. Would you like to come inside?"

She opens the door to her office, and Morgan gives me a thumbs-up. It's a small gesture, but a heartening one, and all I need really, to give me the courage to walk into the office.

17

"I'M AFRAID THE OFFICE IS STILL PRETTY disorganized," the doctor says, flipping on the lights. "Maybe one of these days we'll get things in order around here."

She's right: The office is a mess. I remember my guidance counselor's office; how organized it all was, how in place everything was. Here nothing is in place. I'm not even sure where to sit: There are stacks of manila folders on the chairs, boxes of books on the couch.

"I don't know if my mom told you," I say, "but we're only going to be in Chicago until the trial's over."

"Yes, she mentioned it," the doctor says. She clears off the chairs and drops the folders on her desk.

"I'm just wondering if it's a good idea to start something I won't be able to finish. I mean, I'm only going to be here a few months."

"We can accomplish a lot in a few months. Let's get started, okay?"

She sinks down into one of the chairs and waits for me to sit in the other one. I don't like the way the chairs are positioned: facing each other and just a few feet apart. I can already feel myself freezing up inside.

"I guess I thought I'd have to lie down on a couch," I tell her.

"Do you want to?"

"No, I just thought that's the way it worked. I thought I was supposed to lie down on a couch and bitch about my mother."

"Can't you bitch about her from the chair?" she asks. "I really don't want to have to clear off the couch."

It's hard not to laugh. Okay, so she has a sense of humor. I know just how to finesse someone like her: keep things light and on the surface; the hour will fly by in no time.

"This is going to be so easy for you," I say, sitting in the chair. "I still don't think I belong here, not really, but my mom . . . well, I guess it upset her, you know, when I was in the hospital."

"That was an upsetting night for both of you."

"I guess. Yeah."

"Do you remember what happened when you blacked out?"

"I had . . . it was like a daydream, sort of."

"It wasn't any ordinary daydream, though, was it?"

"No." The fear from that night slams into me again, catching me completely off guard. So much for keeping things light and on the surface. I look at her. "I was inside the daydream. I couldn't control it."

I wait for her to say the words I've heard before—words that don't help at all—words like: "If you just try harder . . . focus . . . stay on task," but she looks at me gravely.

"That must have been terrifying for you," she says.

Only here a few minutes and I'm so blown away because in front of me sits someone who understands how unpredictable and weird my life has suddenly become. "I keep thinking it'll stop, but it doesn't. It's like . . . it's like I get pulled into a dream, only it's not a dream—it's real and I'm trapped inside it and I can't *help* it."

"I know you can't," she says quietly. "You never have any warning that it's going to happen?"

I shake my head.

"When did it start?"

"When we first came here to Chicago. It never happened back home."

She settles back in her chair. "Tell me a little about your life back home in California."

"What do you mean? You want to know what I do each day when I'm back home—stuff like that?"

She nods. I don't get it. What does this have to do with anything?

"My day-to-day life back in California. Okay. Well, this spring I cut so much school I failed my junior year. Is that the kind of stuff you want to know?"

Her eyes get that amused look in them, the same look I remember from the hospital. "When I was talking to you and your mom the other day, I got the feeling you didn't like school too much."

"That's not why I cut."

"Why, then?"

"I wanted to hang out with my friend. I knew we were going to be apart for the summer, and I wanted to spend as much time with him as I could."

"He's the friend you were telling me about in the emergency room?"

"Webb. Yeah."

"Are you very close to him?"

This is getting *way* too personal for me. It's not that I have anything to hide, it's just that some things are private.

"He's just someone I hang out with, that's all. No big deal."

Click, click, click. I can practically hear the wheels turning in her head. It makes me jumpy. "How long have you known him?"

Off limits, I want to scream.

"What difference does it make?" I ask. "I told you: He's just a friend. End of story."

"You don't want to talk about him?"

"It'd be a waste of time."

"Maybe not."

I would like to escape. Just jump out of this chair; run out of the office. Maybe talk Morgan into taking a break, doing something crazy. We could go to a dark bar someplace that has candles in amber glasses and order a couple of drinks and pretend we're two dangerous young women asking for trouble. . . .

I know all about getting into trouble with you, Webb says.

Remember what happened when we sneaked aboard that sight-seeing boat?

I'll never forget the look on your face when we were out on the bay and the guy running the tour realized we hadn't paid our fare.

He was going to call the police when we docked at the wharf.

We were too fast for him, though, I say, laughing. *We made sure we got lost in the crowd when we left the boat. . . .*

"Jamie?" I hear the doctor say. "Are you still with me?"

I'm like a diver who's tried to resurface too fast. It takes me a couple of seconds to look around, to get my bearings, to realize I'm still in the doctor's office, to notice her hand on my shoulder.

"What just happened?" she asks.

"Nothing." I'm sure my face is bright red; I can feel my cheeks burning. "Nothing happened."

The doctor takes her hand from my shoulder and looks at me. "You drifted away from me."

"No, I was just thinking about something. I didn't drift anywhere. I was . . ."

Wow, what a world-class stupid thing to say. I'm sure she doesn't believe me. I don't blame her. The least I could have done was to come up with a better lie. Something a little creative, at least.

She gets up to check the coffee maker. I'm just so relieved we're not sitting face-to-face anymore. I can feel myself start to relax a little.

"Your mom mentioned that it's just been the two of you since your dad died," the doctor says. "Do you get along okay with her?"

"I guess so."

"What about her work on the Renfro trial? How has it affected you?"

"It hasn't."

"Not at all?"

"I've been through it before. This isn't the first high-profile trial she's worked on."

"Coffee?" she asks, and I shake my head. It's not so nerve-wracking now, sitting here, being offered a cup of coffee. "Your mom has worked on a another high-profile trial like this? When?"

"When I was nine. She prosecuted a child molester. The case made her sort of famous; she was on the news a lot that year."

"It sounds like that kind of case would be all-consuming," the doctor says, pouring some coffee into a blue china mug. "Who took care of you while your mom was busy with the trial?"

"Who took care of me?" My mind is an absolute blank. The doctor comes over and sits down. She sips her coffee and waits for me to say something. "I don't know; I don't remember."

"Someone must have looked after you; nine's too young to be on your own."

"I had a baby-sitter, I think." Her face comes swirling back, watery at first, then sharpens into focus. "Ellis," I say, smiling. "I'd forgotten about her."

"Did you like Ellis?"

"I thought she was cool. She was in college, which made her about a hundred years younger than the other baby-sitters I'd had. She was sort of like a big sister to me."

"What happened to her?"

"I don't know. I guess my mom didn't need her after the trial ended. I guess she moved away somewhere."

The doctor sets her coffee down. "Let's stop for today," she says. "I know how hard a first session can be." She goes to her desk and scribbles something on a prescription pad. "I'm going to start you on some medication that'll help take the edge off your anxiety."

I didn't mention I was anxious, but she picked up on it somehow. Or maybe I'm telegraphing things I'm not even aware of.

"Will it stop what happens to me?" I ask. "The daydreams, I mean."

"No. But I think that as we work together, you'll start to regain some control over your inner world."

She hands me the slip of paper and goes out to the waiting room and returns with an appointment book. I can see Morgan bent over the computer keyboard at her desk; she looks up at me and smiles. I smile back, something I'm surprised I can do, considering how I've just had my head cracked open and my brain examined.

"Let's set up our regular sessions for Wednesdays and Fridays," the doctor says, reaching for a pencil. "Is that all right?"

"Twice a week? Why do I have to come twice a week?"

"Well, you mentioned it yourself: you're only here for a few months. We have a lot to do in a short time." She jots my name down in her book. "Is two o'clock okay?"

"I guess so."

Morgan hands me an appointment card on my way out. "I'll talk to you later, okay?" she asks. "Maybe we can do something."

"Maybe tomorrow. I think I just want to go home and lie down for a while. I didn't sleep too well last night."

I don't worry that she won't understand. I know she will.

"Tomorrow," she says.

I stop at the Walgreen's near our apartment and drop off my prescription. It isn't until I'm on my way out of the store that I notice the magazine and newspaper racks—Sally Renfro's face stares at me from the front page of the *Sun-Times*. TESSMAN DETAILS ABUSE, the headline says. I know what a traumatic childhood Sally Renfro had: I've heard my mom talk about it often enough with the other lawyers on the case. I usually clip any news article that mentions my mom, but right now I don't feel like reading about someone's troubled life. I only want to go home and kick off my shoes and collapse on the couch, and that's just what I do. I don't even turn the TV on—I've had enough stimuli for one afternoon; I want to drown in the quiet.

Was it as bad as you thought? Webb asks.

Yes and no. It was work. That was something I didn't figure on it was a lot of work.

Know what I think? I think you should forget about your afternoon with the shrink and come with me. The whales are heading back to Baja; let's go down to the wharf and sneak aboard one of the tour boats.

You go ahead. I'm too tired.

Whatever you want, he says. I watch as he runs off toward the wharf. But you don't know what you're missing, kid!

18

"JAMIE, HOW DID IT GO AT THE DOCTOR'S?" my mom asks. It's a little after five, and she's just come in. I wasn't expecting her home so early; I'm still lounging on the couch. "I thought you were going to call me after your appointment."

"I guess I forgot."

"You *forgot*? Well, how was it? How did it go?"

"Okay, I guess. I like her."

"We're lucky she could take you, darling," my mom says. "She's chief of staff at the hospital, and she doesn't have time to accept every patient who's referred to her."

La-dee-dah, I think. I wonder what it says about me—that such an important doctor has decided to let me cut to the head of the cuckoo line. Maybe it's an indication of how warped I am.

"So it went okay, then?" my mom asks.

"Yeah, fine." I stand up and slide into my shoes. "I have to run down to Walgreen's; I dropped off a prescription, and they told me it'd be ready by five."

"She's putting you on medication?"

"Some sort of antianxiety stuff . . ."

"Oh," my mom says, surprised. "Are you . . . I

wasn't aware that you were suffering from any kind of anxiety."

"I never put a name to it, but yeah, 'anxiety' describes it pretty accurately."

"Jamie," my mom says, all worried and everything, "you know, don't you, that you can tell me what's wrong, whatever it is."

Maybe she means it. Maybe it's even true. But there's a part of me that's all sealed up inside. I can feel it heavy in my chest. I don't like carrying that weight around, whatever it is. I look at my mom.

"I'd tell you if I could," I say. "If I knew what was wrong, I'd tell you."

Breeeeeep. Mom's cell phone. "Dammit," she says, clicking it on. "Hello? Drew, hi—can you hold on a minute?" She presses the MUTE button. "I need to go over some things with Drew, but I should be finished by the time you get back. Maybe we could go out to dinner."

I nod. "I won't be long."

It hits me while I'm on my way to the drugstore: I feel better, sort of. Maybe it's knowing I'll have some time with my mom at dinner, even though it'll no doubt be punctuated by cell phone interruptions about the trial. Maybe it's something else, though: something amazing that happened when I talked to the doctor earlier. She understood how scared I am, how freaked I am that my inner world has started taking me hostage. She *understood.*

It makes me think that no matter what lies ahead, I won't have to handle it alone. Good thing, too. I'm not running my life very well these days. Maybe I should fire myself and let the doctor take over. Someone else needs to be in charge, I think, at heading up the project that is Me.

19

I DREAM ABOUT THE BABY-SITTER THAT night. When I wake up in the morning, the details of the dream float away from me like rose petals, but it makes me think about Ellis. It's so strange; I went for years without thinking about Ellis at all, but ever since my session with the doctor, all sorts of memory fragments have been set in motion. I loved it when Ellis played big sister to me: I can remember her painting my toenails and teaching me her favorite rock songs. I remember how important I felt when she asked me to help her pick out a dress for some big date she had.

"What do you think, Jamie?" she asked. She came out of the dressing room and twirled around in a sparkly blue dress.

"You look just like a movie star," I said.

She laughed and threw her arms around me. "I hope my boyfriend agrees with you." She turned to look at herself in the mirror. "It's the most incredble thing, Jamie, being in love . . . the most incredible thing . . ."

I thought it was so cool that she talked to me like that, like I was a real friend and not just some kid she was paid to look after.

✳   ✳   ✳

"Do you remember Ellis?" I ask my mother at breakfast. She's sitting at the kitchen table, clicking away at her laptop computer. Yellow legal pads are strewn all over the table, scribbled with cryptic notes and stained with coffee-cup rings.

Mom's face hardens. She keeps on typing. "Ellis, the world's worst baby-sitter. Yes, I remember her."

"I thought you liked her."

"No, dear, *you* liked her. I fired her."

"You fired her? Why?"

"Don't you remember the night she forgot to pick you up after your baseball game? My God, she left you all alone in that park for hours. I'm *still* furious about it."

I pour myself some juice and sit at the table. "No, she picked me up. I remember being in the car with her."

"When she dropped you off for the game, maybe, but I was the one who picked you up. I'll never forget how I felt when I saw you all alone on those bleachers. You looked so small and so scared."

"*You* picked me up? What happened to Ellis? I can't believe she just forgot about me."

"She called me with some wild story about her car breaking down out in the middle of nowhere, but I didn't buy it, not for a second."

"Why not?"

Mom looks up from her computer. "I wouldn't give her the night off to spend time with her boyfriend, but she obviously decided to go meet him anyway."

"So you fired her just because she slipped up one night? Mom, that's *way* cold."

"There was more to it than that." She starts tapping away on the keyboard again. "When Ellis first came to work for us, I thought we'd found the perfect sitter. She had a glowing recommendation from her college's child care center where she'd volunteered, and she was wonderful with you; she absolutely adored you. But after she'd been with us about six months, she met some boy, and he quickly became the center of her universe. She gradually became less and less focused on her job, and I had to keep reminding her that she wasn't being paid to hang on the phone for hours with some boy—she was supposed to be spending time with you. I was so disappointed in her: she'd always been so dependable, but she ended up acting like some silly schoolgirl in love."

"Come on, Mom, that's exactly what she was: a college girl who was being swept her off her feet. I mean, everyone's entitled to be a bit scattered when they fall in love."

"Maybe so," my mother says. "But Ellis knew about the threats I'd received because I was prosecuting Carson White. She *knew* I didn't want you playing baseball in the park until the trial was over, but she took you to your game anyway."

"Well, what are you saying? That she ditched me at the game so she could spend time with her boyfriend?"

"It looked that way to me. I can't even *begin* to tell you how upset I was with her. We had the security system at home, but the police didn't think it was wise for you to be out in public alone during that time, and Ellis knew it. Can you blame me for going crazy when I found out that she took you to your game that night and then neglected to pick you up?"

"Well, what happened to her after you fired her? Did she move away somewhere?"

"I really don't know. She always talked about moving to the East Coast when she finished college, so maybe she and her boyfriend ended up back there."

I sit there and drink my juice while Mom works. I try to read her trial notes upside down: the felt-tip scribbles only she can decipher, the abbreviations, the case law she's jotted down. None of it makes sense to me. I feel my thoughts are the same way: chaotic, jumbled. I wonder if I'll ever be able to untangle them, and what I will find when I do.

20

MORGAN AND I ARE IN MY KITCHEN, comparing high school horror stories while I try to teach her how to make a salade Niçoise. I'm afraid the cooking lesson is turning out to be a lost cause, though: Her culinary skills are a bit lacking, and I may have to demote her to table-setter.

"Okay, so you didn't fit in at school," I say, "but I'll bet you were never the target of a clique."

"No, thank God. Why? Were you?"

"There are six weasels at my school masquerading as cheerleaders, and they love nothing better than to torment me."

She arranges lettuce on some plates. "What do they torment you about?"

"Anything. You name it. Webb keeps telling me I don't belong in a snobby prep school, but my mom definitely doesn't agree."

"Doesn't he go there too?"

"No, he's been out of school for a couple of years. I think he's still trying to decide what to do with his life."

"An older man, eh?" She drops some tuna on one of the plates. "Maybe you'd better do this. It's not turning out like the picture in the cookbook."

I arrange the tuna on the plates, add some tomato wedges and olives.

"Where'd you learn all this stuff about cooking?" Morgan asks.

"I sort of picked it up myself . . . my mom says my dad was an amateur chef, though, so maybe it's genetic."

"We don't have any gourmet cooking genes in my family, I don't think."

"What about your aunt?"

"Her idea of cooking is to warm up leftover pizza."

I laugh. "Yeah, I guess she's a little too busy to spend a lot of time cooking." I put our plates on the table. "You were right about her being easy to talk to; I really like her."

"I was hoping you would."

"When you were telling me how she helped pull you out of that black hole or whatever after your friend died . . . well, how did she do it?"

"I'm not sure, exactly," Morgan says. "She's just got a talent for people, I guess. My dad says she was always that way, even as a little kid."

Or maybe it's magic, I think, *and the doctor is my amazing fairy-god-shrink-mother.*

No magic wand at my next session, though, and no fairy dust.

"You'll be happy to know," the doctor says, showing me into her still-cluttered office, "that I cleared off the couch, in case you want to lie down this time."

I like it that she can tease me. "Thanks, but I think I'll just sit in the chair again."

"So," she says, taking the chair facing mine, "I've been thinking about some of the things we talked about last time, and I keep coming back to the night you were taken to the hospital."

"What do you mean?" I ask. "I already told you everything about that night."

"You told me you blanked out, but can you remember what led up to it?"

"What led up to it?"

She nods. "What were you doing before it happened?"

"Morgan and I had dinner—I guess you knew that, though—and . . ." That creepy photo from the Renfro crime scene suddenly pops into my head. I force myself to stay calm and matter-of-fact. "I saw a picture," I say. "It must have fallen out of one of my mom's legal files, and when I went to pick it up, I guess it sent me into shock or something."

"It was a disturbing photograph?"

"Disturbing? Yeah, it was a picture of the Renfro murder scene. I guess I blanked out after I saw it. That can happen, can't it? Something's so creepy that your mind just sort of shuts down and goes blank?"

"The thing is," the doctor says, "when I saw you in the emergency room, you weren't in a blank state of mind at all. You thought you were with your friend Webb, remember?"

I look at her. "I don't want to talk about that night."

Higher, I tell him.

I'm in the park where we met, on the kiddie swings. I have to hold my feet up so they won't drag on the ground as Webb pushes me.

You're not as light as you used to be, you know, he says.

Very funny. Put some muscle into it.

When did you get so demanding, Jamie?

I'm not demanding. I just want my feet to touch the sky. Is that too much to ask for?

All right, he says, pulling the swing chains back as far as they'll go. Prepare to become airborne!

"Jamie?" the doctor says. "*Jamie.*" I'm suddenly jolted out of my surroundings with Webb. "Are you back? Let's talk about what just happened."

I look around the office, look at the doctor, and slowly realize I've left Webb behind. My heart beats wildly and out of control. I can't sort this out. I can't make any sense out of time, distance, and geography.

"I was here the whole time?" I ask.

"The whole time," the doctor says.

"But I was with him," I whisper. "I was really with him."

"Not in the way you think."

"Did I talk to him out loud? Did you hear me?"

"Yes."

This is just too weird for me, having my inner world turn itself inside out and spill all over the place so the doctor can see it.

Suddenly I'm on my feet. "I don't think I can do this."

"Jamie, sit down—"

"I can't deal with this right now—"

"Nothing will get better until you can start telling me about some of the scary things that are happening to you." She holds her hand out, indicating the chair I just jumped out of. "Please."

I sit down; try to steady my breathing. I think of the last few months. I think of my mom and my counselor and teachers. I made sure none of them could see inside me. But there's no hiding from this person—I can see that—there's no hiding here.

"Do you remember talking to Webb the night I was checking you over in the emergency room?" the doctor asks.

"I thought I was with him." My voice is shaky and barely audible. She sits forward a little so she can hear me. "I saw that creepy photograph, then all of a sudden I was back in California with him."

The doctor reaches for a box of Kleenex and hands it to me. It's the first I'm aware that I'm crying. "Did you tell your mom about seeing the photograph?"

"My mom? No. I promised I wouldn't tell her

about seeing stuff like that." I don't know where those words came from. I look at the doctor and try to explain, but I can't.

"Who asked you to make a promise like that?"

"No one." I can feel the cobwebs growing in my head, blotting out my thoughts. "I didn't mean it the way it sounded. I promised myself I wouldn't worry her while she's under so much pressure with the trial."

She leans back in her chair. "You told me at our last session that before you came here, before you came to Chicago, you never daydreamed about Webb."

"I didn't have to. If I wanted to see him, I'd just cut school and meet him down at the beach or the park or Otter Cove."

I'm so worried about what she must think. I wipe my eyes and brace myself for more questions.

"You miss him a lot," the doctor says.

"Yeah, I miss him. I wish I could have gone to Europe with him this summer. He's the only person who understands me and . . ." I stop; try to regroup. "It's like you trick me, sort of, into telling you stuff."

"I'm not trying to trick you," the doctor says. I could fall into her eyes, I'm thinking; they're so dilated, so focused on me. "I need to know a lot. I'm concerned a bit, because Webb seems to have such a grip on you."

"No, not a grip," I tell her. "That sounds bad somehow. It's not like that with Webb and me."

"How long have you known him?"

"Since I was nine. A bunch of us kids from school used to get together after dinner to play baseball, only I lived so far away from the park that Ellis—she was the sitter I told you about— Ellis had to drive me there. One night she forgot to pick me up after my game. I got scared because the field was so deserted, but Webb noticed me when he was taking a shortcut through the woods. He stayed with me and made sure nothing happened to me."

"What would have happened to you if Webb hadn't shown up that night?"

"Nothing." I can't keep the irritation out of my voice. "I was nine years old. I was alone. It was getting dark. You know how kids are: They imagine all sorts of stupid stuff."

"Like what?"

"Like what? You really want to know like what? Okay. I thought I saw Spiderman lurking in the bushes, spying on me. Spiderman. From the comics. God, I can't believe how deranged I sound. I *told* you it was stupid."

She digests all this. I'm wondering what's coming next. A wild pitch out of left field, I'm guessing, and I'm right:

"Did your mom get angry at Ellis?"

"For not picking me up that night, you mean?"

The doctor nods.

"She fired her, I guess." I can't answer any more questions; I just can't. I push myself up from the chair and pace a bit, stopping to look at some of the framed diplomas and important-looking documents that are plastered all over the wall: UNIVERSITY OF ILLINOIS COLLEGE OF MEDICINE, AMERICAN PSYCHIATRIC ASSOCIATION'S OUTSTANDING ACHIEVEMENT AWARD, COOK COUNTY MEDICAL SOCIETY PHYSICIAN OF THE YEAR, AMA RECOGNITION OF CONTINUING EDUCATION.

"I think you're what they call an overachiever," I say, and the doctor bursts out laughing. It's like her laughter lightens everything inside me that is heavy and scared.

"I think you're absolutely right," she says.

I turn around and look at her. "I wanted to ask you . . . I need to know. . . ." It takes me a while to get it out, and she waits, listening intently, until I can say it: "There's something really wrong with me, isn't there?"

She stops smiling and looks at me with great empathy—the way people look when they want to break bad news softly. "I think there's a reason you need to escape into a secret world," she says. "Maybe we can work together and find out what it is."

I push back the fear I'm suddenly feeling. "I'm not ready. I'm not ready for that."

"I know you're not," the doctor says. "It's going to take time."

If that's supposed to make me feel better—well, it doesn't. I don't like playing with fire, flirting with danger, talking about secrets. These things can only lead to disaster. Can't the doctor see that? Someone with so many diplomas should know that; she really should.

21

I'M ALMOST SURE IT'S JUST AN ANIMAL making the bushes rustle, but I'm still scared. There's a full moon tonight, enough light for me to see that I'm the only one here; the only one left on the baseball field. A sudden flash of movement through all the foliage, then, and Spiderman steps out of the woods. Spiderman, from the comics.

"I'm not going to hurt you, Jamie," he says. He has a kind voice, but the words are scary. "Look at you! You look just like a scared little rabbit!"

As he gets closer he transforms himself from Spiderman to an ordinary mortal. He's wearing a hooded red sweatshirt and sunglasses. Sunglasses, even though it's nighttime.

He holds his hand out. "You come with me, darlin'."

I can't move. I'm paralyzed.

"Did you hear what I said?"

He reaches for me, but I take a step backward. I look around for Ellis. For someone. *For anyone.*

"Webb!" I scream. *"Webb!"*

"Jamie? Jamie, wake up. Are you all right?"

I open my eyes, startled, and sit up in bed. The

room's pitch black, and my mom is silhouetted against the light coming from the hall.

"You were having a nightmare," my mother says. "Are you okay? I could hear you all the way across the hall."

"You heard me? What was I saying?"

"I thought you were calling me," she says. She walks over to the bed. "What were you dreaming about? You sounded so frantic."

"Nothing. I don't know. It didn't make any sense."

"You used to have terrible nightmares, do you remember? You used to dream someone was chasing you."

"Yeah. That was a long time ago."

"I used to sit with you until you could go back to sleep."

"I remember."

"Do you want me to stay with you a little while?"

I want that. I want that a lot. But I can't risk it; can't risk falling asleep and having another nightmare and waking up screaming. I don't want my mother to see how crazy I'm becoming.

"I'll be okay, Mom. You'd better get back to bed or you'll be a very tired defense attorney in the morning."

I can't see her face too well, but I know she's smiling. "Are you going to be able to sleep?"

"I think so. Sorry I woke you up."

"Call me if you need me."

As soon as she's gone, I tiptoe out to the kitchen and make a strong cup of coffee. I'm beyond exhaustion, but sipping industrial-strength coffee and staying awake is a lot better than going to sleep and letting my subconscious hijack my brain. Right now I don't plan on sleeping ever again. I wonder how long I'll be able to keep it up, though. People who are sleep deprived, I remember reading somewhere, become a little psychotic.

I'm already a little psychotic, I think, and too numb to care about it.

22

"YOU LOOK TIRED TODAY," THE DOCTOR says at our next session. "Are you feeling all right?"

I sink down into the chair and try to phrase my request just the right way so I can get what I want.

"The Xanax you prescribed isn't helping any," I say. "I was wondering if you could give me something else. Something stronger."

She's over by the windows, getting herself some coffee. "Well, before we think about changing your medication, tell me what the problem is . . ."

"I don't know. I've just been all stressed since I started therapy. It spills over into the rest of the day when I leave here, and I can't turn it off."

"Maybe we should talk about it."

"Talking won't help." I make myself stay calm; I don't want to sound desperate. "I'm nervous and jumpy all the time now. I need something really strong to help me relax."

"I don't think you could get much more relaxed than you are right now," the doctor says. "You look like you're about to go to sleep."

I'm so wracked with fatigue I just sort of crupt.

"God, why can't you just give me a prescription for some medicine that will make me *feel* better? You're my doctor—you're supposed to *help* me!"

She's so damned unflappable. She pours some milk into her coffee, stirs it, then comes over and sits down and looks at me. "What's happened since our last session?" she asks. "What's wrong?"

I have no reserves of energy left. I'm too worn out to invent a story and too tired to storm out of the office.

"A couple of nights ago my mom had to wake me up because I was talking in my sleep. She said I sounded frantic—that was how she described it— *frantic.*"

"Were you having a dream?"

I look at her. "You want to know about my dreams now? What a cliché."

She smiles a little. "You didn't think you could go through therapy without having to tell me a dream or two, did you?"

I close my eyes for a second and try to organize my thoughts.

"It was stupid . . . I was back on the baseball field the night Ellis forgot to pick me up, and this stranger—this person I thought was Spiderman— stepped out of the woods and turned himself into an ordinary person. A person wearing a hooded red sweatshirt and sunglasses."

"Could it be true?"

"It was just a dream."

"Or a memory," she says.

"How could it be a memory? God, I've known Webb how long—eight years. He would have mentioned it if there'd been some stranger hanging around the baseball field that night. He was right there with me. He never left my side; not for a second."

"He wasn't with you the whole time, though, was he? Was he there when your mom picked you up?"

"Yes. No, wait a minute. . . ." It's like the pictures I've had in my head about that night are suddenly rushing to rearrange themselves. "Maybe he left when my mom . . ." I can feel the room start to tip and sway. "I have blank spots about that night. I just remember how scared I was before he came. How I jumped at every little noise I heard." I see myself at nine years old, alone on the baseball field, watching the woods. Waiting.

"What is it?" the doctor asks.

"I picked up a stick that night," I hear myself say. "I picked up a stick and held it tight, as tight as I could."

"Why?"

"It was my weapon."

"Why did you need a weapon?"

"I can *feel* it. I can feel it in my hand right now. I remember how heavy it was, how my fingers curled around it, how I wouldn't let go of it. I remember the burn I got when it was pulled out of my hand—"

"Jamie, *careful*! You're hurting yourself." The

doctor reaches for my right hand, clenched so tightly my nails are digging into my flesh. "Open your hand; let me see."

I just sit there, too stunned at first to feel any pain, too much in shock to realize that I've inflicted these bleeding crescent-shaped wounds on myself.

The doctor presses some Kleenex into my hand. "Who pulled the stick away from you?"

I shake my head. "I don't know."

"Someone strong—"

"I don't remember."

"Look how tightly you were holding on to it—"

"I said I don't remember! I don't remember *who* pulled the stick away from me! Maybe no one did! Maybe I've got it all mixed up with some movie I saw!"

I slump down in the chair. I feel like hell. I can't wait till this session is over.

There's a long stretch of quiet. The doctor goes over to the bookcase beneath the windows and gets her medical bag. "Do you ever talk to your mom about how frightened you were that night?"

"Why should I? She knows I was scared because Ellis didn't show up. What's there to talk about?"

I'm careful not to make eye contact with her when she comes back. It's all starting to sink in now: how shrill my voice has been this session, how sarcastic and rude I've sounded. I don't know what's happening to me; I just don't know.

"Let's see if I can impress you with the medical skills I learned back when I was an intern," the doctor says. She takes my hand and cleans it off with an antiseptic wipe. "You know, all patients resist getting close to things that are scary. That's your job, in a way—to protect yourself from getting hurt."

I look at her now. "I'm just not sure I'm strong enough for all this."

"That's why I'm here," the doctor says. "To keep you from falling too far, too fast."

I take a deep breath. "Okay, there's something I have to tell you. Something I think you should know. My mom says . . . she says she got some threatening mail during the time she was prosecuting the child abuse case. She told Ellis she didn't want me playing baseball in the park until the trial was over, but Ellis had a date that night so she took me to my game anyway. She forgot to pick me up when it was over. She forgot all about me and never came."

I'm hoping she doesn't make me talk more about it, because I can't. I won't. She glances at me briefly, then finishes taping a square of gauze to my hand. "You're exhausted," she says. "Go home and get some rest. You've earned it; you've accomplished a lot today."

It's true: I'm bone-tired, and not just from the lack of sleep. I've given it all to the doctor—all the tension and fear I carried in here. I'm not used to the sense of well-being I suddenly possess. I know it won't last, but I don't care. After the emotional roller coaster I've been riding lately, I'll take what comfort I can get, no matter how temporary it may be.

23

FOR THE NEXT FEW DAYS I FLOAT around the city in a bubble of serenity. No nightmares. No black cloud hovering over me. Being freed from my recent crazed-out nuttiness has let me get back to the ordinary business of being a seventeen-year-old citizen of the planet Earth. I cook up a storm for my mom, catch some of the trial down at the courthouse, and, like today, hang out with Morgan. That's the best part, really—having a pal here in the city who wants to spend time with me.

"I *hate* the mirrors in these dressing rooms," Morgan says. "I mean, let's face it: They were designed by sadists."

"Yeah, do we really need to see every single body flaw from three different angles?" I ask.

We're in adjoining dressing rooms at the department store, Morgan and I. She's the one doing the serious shopping; I'm just getting a pair of jeans. I know it's not such an amazing thing to go shopping with a girlfriend, but I'm having the time of my life. Just a few short days ago I was afraid I was becoming a serious head case, and now it looks like my brain is finally getting back on track.

"Okay," Morgan calls over the dressing room wall partition, "I've had it with this torture. I'll meet you out front."

"Which skirt are you getting?"

"The black one. I figure it'll make me look thinner."

"You know, guys never worry about stuff like that—"

"About how they look in skirts? No, probably not."

"Cut it out!" I say, laughing. "I mean they don't obsess about their weight the way we do."

We walk back to my apartment, just two victims of the fashion system.

"This little skirt-buying excursion was my mom's idea," Morgan says. "Last night she called from Gourdon, France, and told me I'd better start getting a few 'nice' things for my freshman year at college. And I reminded her that it's a theater school, and also not the 1800s, and that nobody on campus is going to be wearing skirts."

"They all do it, you know. The nagging, I'm talking about. It'd be weird if they didn't. I mean, think about it: What would we do if they *stopped* nagging?"

"Faint," she says.

❋   ❋   ❋

This perfect afternoon starts disintegrating as soon as Morgan and I walk into the apartment. A chain of events is set into motion with a simple phone call from my mom:

"Jamie, I'm so glad you're home. Listen, darling, I forgot one of my legal files. It should be on the table by the front door."

I spot the thick manila folder on the table. "Yeah, I see it . . . do you want me to bring it over to the courthouse?"

"No, one of the other lawyers will pick it up; I'll have him meet you down in front of the building in a few minutes, all right? Thanks, dear; you're a lifesaver."

Click.

"My mom forgot one of her legal files," I tell Morgan as I hang up the phone. "I was going to make us something fantastic for lunch, but I guess it'll have to wait."

"You're going over to the courthouse?"

"Just downstairs. One of her colleagues is coming by to pick it up."

It starts out okay. It starts out fine. We wait in front of my apartment building and make exceptionally witty and cutting remarks about everyone who walks into the lobby. As a few minutes pass, though, I keep my eyes glued to the street. I don't want to get distracted and somehow miss my mom's colleague. I'm guessing he'll pull up in a yellow

Checker cab, and he does, eventually. The taxi stops right in front of our building, and the young lawyer gets out. I remember seeing him the night all the lawyers came over to the apartment to discuss the trial.

"Jamie?" he says, smiling. "Stuart Novy; we've met before, I believe. Is that your mom's file?"

He reaches for the file I'm holding, but I back away from him.

No.

No.

No.

I don't like it when someone tries to pull something out of my hands.

I hold on to the stick tight, as tight as I can, but he yanks it away from me. The palm of my hand burns, but I don t look at it; I don t dare take my eyes off him.

You come with me, darlin, he says.

I can t move.

I m paralyzed.

Did you hear what I said? Get over here.

Now.

"Is there a problem?" this Stuart person is saying. He looks so bewildered. "Your mother told you I'd be coming by for the file, right?"

"Jamie, are you okay?" Morgan whispers. "What's wrong?"

"I'm in a bit of a hurry," Stuart says. "The cab's waiting, as you can see, so if I can just have the file . . ."

He takes a step forward and reaches for the manila folder, and I drop it, just drop it, and the papers fly out of it and swirl up around us like oversized confetti.

"Jamie, what's wrong?" Morgan asks.

I turn around and run back into the building, into an empty elevator. Morgan's right behind me.

"Jamie, what *is* it?"

"I don't like it when someone tries to grab something out of my hands like that."

"Jamie, he didn't try to grab the file out of your hands."

I can't punch the elevator buttons. My fingers are shaking too hard.

"I want to go back to the apartment." I can hardly speak. "Just take me back to the apartment."

She looks plenty panicked. "Okay, it's all right; just hold on." She punches the button and I do hold on, just barely, till we get back to the apartment. As soon as we're inside I sink down onto the couch and bury my head in my hands.

"Don't ask me why I freaked out down there, because I don't *know.*"

"I won't. I won't ask you about it."

"God, when he gets back to the courthouse and tells my mom how I flipped out . . ."

"Jamie, your mom won't care about that—"

"But I don't want her to know how crazy I'm getting; how . . ." I look at her. She's shaken up too. "You'll probably run home and tell your aunt all about this, right?"

"No," Morgan says, sitting next to me. "She wouldn't let me, even if I wanted to. She gave me this big lecture before your first appointment . . . all about ethics and privacy."

"Every time I think I'm getting better, something slams into me and knocks me down."

"One step forward, two steps back."

I nod. "Is that the way it was for you after your friend died?"

"Yeah. It's still a struggle. I mean, I don't believe in all that crap about closure. There's always going to be a huge hole in my life because he's gone."

"What was he like?"

"Oh," she says, smiling. "He was really smart and funny and talented . . . he was a professional dancer in lots of musicals here in the city."

"Is that how you got interested in acting?"

"Yeah, I never would have tried out for anything if he hadn't encouraged me. . . . I guess you can tell I was really dependent on him."

"Like I am with Webb," I say. I can feel myself calming down inside. The crazies are slowly leaving, and I'm getting back to my old self. "Believe it or not, I was pretty normal before this summer, before Webb and I were separated. If you had met

136

me a couple of months ago, you would have seen a pretty sane person."

Morgan laughs. "How dull."

"Come on. You're saying you *like* hanging out with someone who's demented?"

"I could ask you the same thing."

"You seem pretty normal."

"That's just my cover," she says. "Hey, do you think you can be demented and cook at the same time? I could really go for that fantastic lunch you were talking about earlier."

"Oh, I get it. An ulterior motive for making me feel better." I get up and go to the kitchen. "What are you going to be doing while I demonstrate my amazing culinary talent?"

"I'll sit at the table and offer unsolicited cooking tips."

"Gee, thanks."

"Don't mention it," she says, grinning. "What are friends for?"

24

"MOM?"

We've finished dinner and she's sitting on the couch, her laptop computer balanced on her knees as she looks through some of her files.

"Can I bring Morgan down to the courthouse sometime?" I ask. "I think it'd be interesting for her to see some of the trial."

"Anytime," my mom says, leafing through her legal pad. "Maybe you'd like to bring her tomorrow; there are some important witnesses scheduled to testify."

I sit down next to her. "Mom, I'm sorry about what happened earlier today with your colleague," I say, and she looks up at me, surprised.

"Darling, I told you, it's all right. Anyone can have a panic attack. Maybe you should talk to the doctor about it." She starts typing on the laptop. "I had something similar happen to me when I was studying for the bar exam . . . too much pressure or something. And your dad was away on a construction job; that didn't help any."

"Dad worked on a construction job? When?"

"Before we were married. I've told you that, I'm sure I have. He worked construction jobs all the time to put himself through law school."

"No, I don't think you ever told me that . . . if you told me, I don't remember."

"That was a hard summer for me. He and I were going to backpack through Europe, but at the last minute I decided not to go."

"How come you didn't go with him?"

"Oh," she says, "I was afraid I'd never pass the bar exam if I didn't prepare for it full time. Now I wish I hadn't been quite so driven."

Of course, she's *still* driven. She's not even here right now; she's gone: wrapped up in the Renfro trial. I watch her fingers fly over the keyboard.

"Mom, sometimes I think . . . sometimes I think I'm getting worse."

What I'm saying gets through to her, and she looks at me. "What do you mean? Because of the panic attack you had earlier?"

"I shouldn't have described it as a panic attack. There was more to it than that—"

The phone rings. I'm hoping she'll just let the machine get it. If I don't talk to her now, I never will. I can't stay brave for very much longer, and I'm ready now—right now and only now—to tell her about some of the scary things that have been happening to me lately.

Just let the machine get it, I think.

She reaches for the phone. "Hello? Drew, hi . . . I was just working on it—no, we really need to go over it before tomorrow . . . fine. I'll see you there." Mom hangs up the phone. "Jamie, I'm sorry, darling. Do you want to come with me? We can talk on the way over to the office."

"No, it can wait. I'm tired; I don't really feel like going out anywhere."

"Are you sure?" She closes her laptop and stuffs some papers into her briefcase. "I shouldn't be too late. Maybe we can talk when I get back."

"Okay," I say, but I don't feel brave anymore. I won't try talking to her again, not later or anytime else.

When my mom is gone I curl up on the couch and watch some TV. I click right past the news shows that tell about the Renfro trial and settle on a really bad black-and-white *Creature Feature* movie. While Godzilla munches down Tokyo, I think about some of the things my mom told me. I try to picture her as a young woman who was smitten—that's the word for it, I think—with my dad, like I am with Webb. She and my dad ended up together, though; I'm not so sure Webb and I will have such a happy ending. It's not like he made me any promises about our future the last time I saw him.

He'll be home from his European adventure at the end of summer. I'll be home too, if the stupid trial is over by then. I'm hoping we'll pick up right where we left off. I don't think it's any coincidence that I started going crazy the minute he and I were separated. I just have a feeling that all the strange things that are happening to me will stop once I can see him again, once he wraps his arms around me and we're finally back together again.

25

WE'RE SEATED THREE ROWS BACK, MORGAN and I. The courtroom's enormous, but we're close enough to see Sally Renfro blink back tears as her mother answers questions on the witness stand:

"Mrs. Renfro," my mom says, "what happened when you walked into your house on April twentieth of last year?"

"I saw my husband . . . I saw my husband lying on the floor in a pool of blood."

"Tell the jury what else you saw."

For a second it looks like Sally Renfro's mother is about to fall apart. She struggles to get each word out. "My daughter Sally," she says, "standing over my husband . . . she was holding a gun."

"Did she say anything to you?"

"She said . . . she said, 'He won't hurt either of us again, Mom.'"

The testimony sends chills through me; I look around, wondering if everyone else feels as cold as I do.

"No further questions," my mom says. She sits at the table with Sally Renfro and whispers something to her. I know my mom totally believes Sally Renfro was driven to murder by an abusive step-

father—she wouldn't have come all this way to
take the case if she hadn't—but I wonder if the girl
could be fooling my mom in some way. Anyone
can be fooled, I think. Anyone.

> *Webb? Tell me again about the night we met.*
> *He smiles. You were nine years old, he*
> *says. The tone in his voice is just right: warm*
> *and low. And one night, while I was taking a*
> *shortcut through the woods, I noticed you all*
> *alone on the baseball field.*
> *I was scared because my baseball game*
> *had been over for hours and my mom was so*
> *late picking me up. You told me not to worry.*
> *You told me you'd look after me, remember?*

"You'll have to leave," the bailiff is saying to
me. At first all I can see is his uniform, the gun in
his holster. Then I look around: every single person
in the courtroom is staring at me. Mom's cool
lawyer demeanor is shattered—she's absolutely
horrified. Morgan takes my arm.

"We'll go," she says. "Come on, Jamie."

I let her lead me out into the hall. I'm vaguely
aware of my mom's voice in the background:
"Your Honor, I'd like to request a five-minute
recess. Personal business."

There are reporters outside the courtroom. They
scan our faces and try to decide if we're connected
with the trial, if we're worth pursuing. As soon as

we're away from the crowd, I start to lose it. I clutch at her, at Morgan: "I was daydreaming. Did I do it out loud? Did everyone *hear* me? Did my *mom*?"

"Yeah, I guess everyone heard you," she says, a sympathetic look on her face. "But maybe they thought you and I were talking. I don't think they knew what was really happening."

This is just too much for me to handle. I turn to the wall so she can't see me. I won't fall apart here. I just won't.

"This is personal business," I hear my mom say. "Please turn the camera off; this has nothing to do with the trial . . . Jamie? What was that all about in there? Are you all right?"

I turn around and look at her. "Mom, I'm sorry. I didn't mean to—I'm so sorry."

She holds me at arm's length and looks at me. "That was one of those episodes, wasn't it, that the doctor told us about. One of those episodes that landed you in the hospital."

"Mom, what about the trial? Did you get in trouble because of me?"

She looks over my shoulder at Morgan. "Do you think your aunt could see Jamie this afternoon? Now?"

I hate the tone of urgency in my mother's voice.

"She's probably still at the hospital," Morgan says. "I can have her paged."

"Would you?" my mother asks, relieved, and Morgan nods and heads off down the hall.

"Mom, that was so unnecessary! It could have waited until my next appointment!"

"This can't wait," my mother says.

"Right," I tell her. "Make me feel like an even bigger freak than I am. Get me cured real fast so I don't disrupt any more trials."

Ugly words that hang there. Under normal circumstances we'd probably sit down and talk it over, but the bailiff has just stepped out into the hall:

"Court's reconvening, Mrs. Tessman."

My mom thanks him and starts for the courtroom, then turns around, angrier than I've seen her in a long time: "Don't you *ever* call yourself a freak again."

26

I WANT MORGAN TO COME INTO THE office for my session, but the doctor says no, and banishes her to the waiting room. It's not fair: I could really use some moral support right now. The truth is, I'm not here because I want to be, or need to be, I'm here for my mom, and that's it.

"What happened?" the doctor asks, shutting the door. She must have arrived just before Morgan and I did; she's carrying her medical bag and purse.

"Nothing much." I sink down into the chair. "I just flipped out and made a big scene in court, that's all. You'll probably hear about it on the news."

"Was it another daydream about Webb?"

"Wow, that's so incredibly brilliant."

The doctor sighs and drops her stuff on the desk. "I know you don't want to be here," she says. "This session is your mom's idea, isn't it?"

It hurts. I'm thinking maybe I got my mom into trouble at the trial, and it hurts.

"Just let it go, Jamie," the doctor says, looking at me in such a way that I have no control, no choice in keeping any of it inside.

"Everyone in the courtroom was staring at me,"

I say, trying to keep my voice steady. "I stopped the whole *trial*. The judge could cite my mom for that. It was awful—she even had to ask for a recess so she could come running after me."

"What happened when she did?" the doctor asks, handing me some Kleenex.

"We had this fight because I didn't want to come here." I'm so tired. I press the tissues against my eyes. "Morgan was the only one in the courtroom who didn't make me feel like I was crazy. She always treats me like I'm normal. Like I'm not—I don't know—warped."

The doctor smiles. "Morgan doesn't think you're warped. She thinks of you as a close friend, you know."

"I've never had a close friend, really, except . . . well, except Webb." I wipe my eyes. "I keep thinking they'll stop, but they don't. The daydreams, I mean. They're getting worse."

She sits on the edge of her desk and looks at me. "Jamie, do you remember telling me that the day dreams about Webb didn't start until this summer?"

"They didn't start until we came here to Chicago."

"I think they probably started long before that," she says. "I think they actually started years ago."

"No, I told you: I didn't daydream about Webb when I was back home. I didn't have to. We were together every day."

"Do you think it's possible that some of the times you were with Webb—at the park or the beach or Otter Cove—do you think maybe you were really alone some of those times?"

"No!" I start shredding my wet Kleenex into tiny pieces. "I remember one time—one time we sneaked aboard a sight-seeing boat and pretended we were tourists. I didn't daydream that—it was *real*."

"I think you *wanted* it to be real."

I want her to shut up. I don't want her to say another word.

"Jamie," she says quietly. "Maybe all of those wonderful memories you have of Webb aren't really memories at all. . . ."

I won't listen to this. I won't.

"—maybe they're all elaborate daydreams you've created."

Boom! I hear the explosion in my head, like a bomb detonating, or TNT blowing my whole world apart.

"No! I've known Webb for years—ever since I was nine! He and I have a life together!"

"I wonder if he has a special kind of life, though," the doctor says. "A life you give him."

"Why would I do something like that! I'd have to be really sick, wouldn't I, to . . . to . . ."

"You'd have to be troubled."

"Crazy, you mean!"

"Troubled."

"Troubled about *what*?"

"That's what we're trying to find out." Her total attention is on me, and I'm powerless in the face of it. "I want you to have a life beyond your inner world, Jamie. Beyond Webb."

I suddenly see a flash—a split-second movie frame—of a man walking onto the baseball field; a man wearing a hooded red sweatshirt and sunglasses.

"You don't know what you're talking about." I jump out of the chair and head for the door. "You don't know *anything*."

Maybe she says something, maybe she doesn't. I don't wait to hear. I don't stop to look at Morgan as I run through the waiting room. I'm not coming back here. I don't care what my mom says.

I'm not coming back.

27

I CHECK THE ANSWERING MACHINE WHEN I get home. As soon as I hear the doctor's voice: "Jamie, this is Dr. Hackett . . ." I press the DELETE button. I won't let myself think of what happened earlier at my session. I'll just file it away in the back of my head somewhere. Once it's locked away, it can't hurt me.

At five o'clock, I flip on the news. The report from the courthouse isn't as bad as I thought it would be: there's a mention of a "brief disturbance during the Renfro trial," but that's it—no video of me or anything, no announcement that it was the daughter of the lead defense attorney who brought the wheels of justice to a screeching halt.

"Jamie?"

I turn around to face my mom. She lingers just inside the apartment door and studies me—who knows what she's searching for? Signs of mental collapse, no doubt.

"How come you're home so early?" I ask.

My mother frowns. "I just got a call from the doctor; she's very concerned about you—"

"She called you? Why?"

"*Why?* She said you cut your session short. She wants to see you tomorrow at four—"

"Forget it. I'm not going back there."

"What do you mean you're not going back there?" my mom asks.

"The whole thing is a big waste of time. She isn't helping me at all."

"What did she say about that episode you had earlier today?"

"Didn't she tell you?"

"No." She folds her arms and pins me to the wall with an icy stare. I've seen her act like this in court, and the person on the witness stand usually buckles under the pressure. "Jamie, I thought you liked her—"

"Look, she doesn't know what she's talking about! It's not working, and I don't want to back there!"

"You have to see *someone,*" my mom says. "If you really don't like Dr. Hackett, we'll find someone else."

"When we get back to California."

"No. Now."

"Mom, why are you *doing* this to me?"

"What kind of parent would I be if I didn't get you help when you needed it?"

I don't have an answer for that.

"I saw a psychiatrist once, did you know that?" she asks. "Right after your dad died. I was overwhelmed with it all—losing him, and faced with the prospect of raising my three-and-a-half-year-old all by myself."

"You went to a shrink? Did it help?"

"Eventually."

"I think about it sometimes; how hard it's been for you to handle everything alone."

"We've managed, haven't we?"

"I guess. Yeah."

All during dinner we're careful not to bring up the doctor business again, but I know my mom won't let it drop, and she doesn't. As I start to clear the table, she puts her hand on my arm.

"We have to settle it," she says.

"Mom . . ."

"Now."

There's no point in trying to argue with someone as skilled at verbal jousting as she is. It's just easier to cave in and agree with her.

"Okay," I say, after a moment. "Okay, I'll stay in therapy."

"She wants to see you tomorrow at four," my mom says. "You'll keep the appointment, won't you?"

"Yeah, I'll keep the appointment."

My mom nods, satisfied, and starts unloading her briefcase for her court homework. I don't know where I'll be tomorrow at four, but it sure as hell won't be the doctor's office. I've had it with therapy. No more doctor for me.

My mom picks up the phone and makes the first of what will probably be a zillion phone calls before the evening is over. "Drew, hi . . . I didn't get a chance to talk to you before I left today. Let me look through my notes. . . ."

"I'm going to pick up a few things for breakfast at the corner market," I whisper. "Do you want anything?"

She shakes her head; covers the phone with one hand. "Do you need money?"

"No, I'm fine. Be back in a few minutes."

I buy some bread and coffee and grapefruit juice at the market, then as I'm walking home I hear the far-off voices of kids cheering and yelling. It must be a neighborhood baseball game—there's no mistaking the sound of a bat as it cracks against the ball—and I follow the racket till it gets louder and louder, till I turn a corner and discover a wonderful grassy park in the middle of the urban sprawl. I stand on the sidewalk and watch a bunch of kids waving good-bye to each other as they run off the field. I'm disappointed that the game's over; I wish I could have seen some of it. The kids are breathless and laughing as they head for home. There's something about the angle of the setting sun and the empty field that leaves me with a strange, uneasy feeling. . . .

You remember how it was that night after your baseball game, Jamie, Webb says. You remember hearing the footsteps. You remember seeing him.

When I first heard the footsteps, I hoped it was someone I knew. The baby-sitter who was supposed to pick me up, maybe, or one of the kids from my baseball game.

It wasn't anyone you knew, Jamie. You didn't know him at all, but he knew you. He'd been watching you.

He tried to make me go with him. He tried to make me go with him, but you stopped him.

Webb shakes his head. I wasn't there.

He didn't take me! You were there to stop him!

No, Webb says in a weary voice, no one was there to stop him.

I was only nine years old! I was only nine! I needed someone to help me!

Webb seems not to hear me. He's standing near the bushes, and the closer I get to him, the deeper into the green he goes.

I still need you! I yell, running after him till I'm in the middle of the thicket. Dark and overgrown, it suddenly seems to possess an eerie, Wonderland aura about it. Webb!

This is where we part company, I'm afraid, he calls. He's so far ahead of me, I can barely see him. So long, Jamie. You'll have to find your own way out....

He s gone. There s no point in going after him. He s gone, and I know I ll never see him again.

"Hey, you guys, wait for me!" someone is saying, and my vision suddenly clears and I realize I'm not in the woods at all, but standing in the deserted park here in Chicago. One of the kids from the baseball game runs to catch up with a couple of her friends, and I watch as they cross the street together.

It wasn t anyone you knew, Jamie. You didn t know him at all, but he knew you. He d been watching you.

I drop the groceries. The bottle of grapefruit juice shatters on the cement, and I turn and start running. Something terrible is going to happen, and I have to get back to the apartment, back to my mom. My lungs burn and my legs ache, but I keep running as hard as I can. I don't think I can outdistance the fear any longer and I don't want to be here, out in public, when it finally catches up with me and I fly completely apart.

28

I WAS NINE YEARS OLD THE FIRST TIME I saw him. I knew right away I was in the company of someone special. Soul mate, confidant, best friend: I knew he'd be all of those things, and over the years it turned out to be true.

"Mom . . ." I stand just inside the door. I can't catch my breath. "Mom, help me . . ."

She looks at me, alarmed. "Jamie, what's wrong?"

"I can't get the blood out of my shirt . . ."

She stands up, the papers in her lap sliding to the floor.

You were nine years old the first time I saw you, I remember Webb telling me. *And one night, while I was taking a shortcut through the woods, I noticed you all alone on the baseball field.*

"Jamie," my mom says, "Jamie, I just talked to the doctor; she's going to meet us at the emergency room."

"No, I want to stay here."

"You can't, darling. You can't stay here."

It is dark and cool here, here inside my closet. I can't catch my breath and soon my heart will explode, but it's safer here than it is anywhere else.

"Jamie, she wants us to come to the hospital. She wants to make sure you're all right—"

"What if she sees the blood on my shirt?"

"Jamie," my mother says in weak voice, "there's no blood on your shirt. Please, darling, please just come with me. . . ."

My mom's cell phone *breeps* out in the living room. I wait for her to go answer it, but she stays right here. She takes my hand, and I don't have the energy to resist her. I feel like a little kid whose mother is walking her to kindergarten on the first day of school.

Taxi ride. The driver's eyes panic in the rearview mirror. He's freaked because I'm trembling and breathing so fast. He steps on the accelerator. A fast left turn into the hospital's curved driveway, then, and an abrupt stop in front of the entrance to the emergency room.

Inside, my mom talks to someone at the admitting desk, and almost right away a nurse walks over to us. "Mrs. Tessman? Dr. Hackett's on her way in; I'll take Jamie back and get her settled."

"Will I be able to see my daughter before she's taken to the psychiatric ward?" my mom asks.

"What?" I pull away from my mother. "You didn't tell me they were going to put me in the psychiatric ward! You didn't tell me!"

"Jamie, honey, please—"

"You didn't *tell* me!"

I turn around and head for the sliding glass doors, and suddenly the nurse is at my side.

"It's okay," she says, reaching for me. "Just come with me; no one's going to hurt you."

Liar. People who say that they aren't going to hurt you are liars.

I shove her away and almost make it to the doors before the nurse and a couple of other angels-of-mercy catch up with me. As soon as they put their hands on me, I start kicking. "She needs to be in a four-point restraint," I hear Dr. Hackett say, and before I know it, I'm lifted up onto a gurney, my wrists and ankles strapped down. I can only lie there and watch the ceiling tiles blur as I'm whisked through the ER and into one of those little patient cubicles.

Dr. Hackett hurries in, her face full of concern and empathy. Her eyes are not frightened like my mother's, or panicked like the taxi driver's. "Jamie, I'm sorry you've had such a rough night."

I look up at her and it's like everything inside me suddenly breaks loose. "I don't want to be put in the psychiatric ward!"

"I know you don't," she says, touching my face. She turns to the nurse: "Two milligrams lorazepam IV."

"Dr. Hackett, *please* don't make me stay here." I pull at the restraints on my wrists, but they hold firmly and there's nothing I can do. Nothing at all. "Please just let me go home."

"No. You need to be here in the hospital, Jamie."

"Something's going to happen. . . ." I'm gulping air and crying so hard I wonder if the doctor can understand me. "Something terrible. I have to get out—"

"Right now you need to rest," the doctor says, pushing up my sleeve. She tears open an alcohol prep packet. "I'm going to give you a shot, Jamie . . . just a little sedation to help you feel quieter inside."

The nurse hands her something and I catch the glimpse of a needle—a hypodermic needle.

"Please, I have to get out," I whisper. "Something terrible is going to happen—"

"No, you're safe here," the doctor says. She pops the cap off the hypodermic. "Okay, Jamie, this is going to sting." The needle slides under my skin, and it burns—it burns so much, then in an instant I'm sinking, falling in slow motion, like Alice down the rabbit hole.

"Dr. Hackett?" The nurse's voice echoes from far away. "I've got the psych unit on hold. They need to know which part of the ward you want Jamie admitted to—"

"The secured unit," the doctor says. She unfastens the straps around my wrists. "Let's free you up a bit here, Jamie."

"What's secured?" I ask. I'm so drugged it's hard to get the words out. "Locked? Does it mean locked?"

She puts her hand on mine. "Yes," she says. "It means locked."

That's the last thing I remember before I sleep. The last thing.

29

MY MIND FLOATS FROM THE DRUG THE doctor gave me, but still I'm aware of my mom's presence, of the light touch of her fingers as she brushes some hair out of my eyes.

"What time is it?" I ask.

"It's late. The doctor's just letting me see you for a minute before I go home."

"I don't need to be here, Mom."

"We'll talk about it tomorrow. Go back to sleep."

I close my eyes. When I open them again, I open them to the stark reality of daylight. It's bad enough to find myself in this hospital room— minus my clothes and outfitted in a baggy white gown and robe—but there's a steel grill on the window. I can't take my eyes off it. It's not one of those decorative grills you see on fancy homes designed to keep burglars *out*; this grill is ugly, its purpose simple: to keep someone like me *in*.

"You're awake."

Morgan sits across the room, her feet tucked up under her.

I sit up in bed. "They let you in?"

"I talked one of the student nurses I know into unlocking the unit door at the end of the hall so I could sneak onto the ward. I guess visitors are sort of off limits, except for your mom."

"So I'm really locked in?"

"Yeah, but so am I."

That makes me smile a little. "You know about what happened last night?"

She nods. "I was the one who answered the phone when your mom called."

"I put on quite a show in the emergency room."

"I've put on a few shows of my own." She scooches her chair over. "So. Really. How are you?"

"Scared."

"It'll be okay."

"I wish I could believe that."

"Is there anything I can do?"

"Not unless you can get me out of here some-how."

"You'll get yourself out."

"I don't know how."

"Yeah, you do. Deep down."

"Everything's turned upside down, Morgan. I feel like I'm living inside *Alice in Wonderland*."

"Wrong kids' book, Jamie," she says. "You're not Alice. You're more like Dorothy in *The Wizard of Oz*. You already have the power to get home—you just don't know it yet."

"My first night here in Chicago I felt like I'd been transported to Oz, so maybe I *am* Dorothy." I dangle my legs over the edge of the bed. "No ruby slippers to click together, though."

She laughs. "I'll go shopping for you and see what I can find."

A nurse steps into the room—a cheerful-looking, grandmotherly type. "Morgan Hackett . . . how on earth did you get in here?"

"Time to go, I guess," Morgan says. "This is Mrs. Getz, Jamie. Don't let her boss you around too much."

"You'll have to wait for me to escort you out of the unit," the nurse says. "I'll just be a minute."

"I'll see you, Jamie, okay?" Morgan says. She gives me an encouraging smile; then she disappears out into the hall.

"Well," the nurse says. "I didn't realize you and Morgan were friends." She comes over and wraps my arm for a blood pressure reading. "How do you feel this morning?"

How do I feel? Too scared to talk. Too scared to think. I try to calm down; I don't want the numbers to give me away.

"Dr. Hackett was here earlier, checking on you," she says. "She thought you might sleep for a couple more hours."

"Do you know if I can go home today?" I ask. "I don't think I need to be here, not really."

The nurse has a kind face, but it's clear she's heard it all before. "You'll have to talk to the doctor about it," she says. "You'll be seeing her later this morning."

My mom comes into the room and waits while

the nurse finishes with me. She looks so rumpled and worried—I wonder if she slept at all last night.

"A little high," the nurse says, ripping the blood pressure cuff off my arm. "Not so surprising, though. This isn't the most relaxing place to wake up in, is it?" She turns to my mom. "Did you find the doctor's office all right?"

My mother nods. "We talked last night, but I still had . . ."—Mom's voice sort of falters—"there were some things I wanted to ask her."

"She's one of the best doctors I've ever worked with," the nurse says, as if answering an unasked question of my mother's. "Your daughter's in good hands."

"Thank you." Mom seems so grateful for any little scrap of reassurance, it almost makes me cringe. When the nurse leaves, Mom doesn't come over and hug me like I'm expecting. She just stares at me. I would almost swear she doesn't recognize me.

"Mom, please don't look at me that way. I don't belong here. This whole thing is a big mistake."

"Jamie, it's not a mistake—"

"I broke the rules when I started talking to the doctor. I broke the rules, and now everything is falling apart."

My mother looks at me, puzzled. "Rules? *What* rules?"

I slide out of bed and walk over to her. "Mom, take me out of this place. The doctor will let me out if you say so. Please just take me *out* of here."

"No." She holds my face in her hands. She looks so scared. I hate it that she's scared, that I'm the cause of it. "The doctor says this is a crucial time for you. It's important for you to be here, where you're safe."

"Where I'm locked up, you mean." I pull away from her and look in the closet, then start flinging open the drawers to a small dresser, where I find my jeans and shirt and socks. "Am I supposed to feel honored or something to have such a *genius* of a doctor working on me? Because I don't."

My mother sighs. "Maybe you should."

There's a tap on the door, and the nurse sticks her head in. "Mrs. Tessman, I'm sorry, but it's time for you to leave."

"Yes, I know; I'll just be a minute." Mom turns to me. "Honey, the doctor doesn't want me to visit again until you've had a chance to get settled here—"

"I can't wear this." I hold up my shirt. "Look . . ."

My mother frowns. "Jamie, not the shirt again—"

"It's still spattered with blood."

"Jamie," she says, "I told you last night: There isn't any blood on that shirt—"

"There's blood all over it!" I hurry into the bathroom and turn the water on full blast. I try to wash the stain out of the shirt with some liquid soap from the built-in dispenser.

My mother stands in the bathroom doorway.

"Jamie, there's nothing on the shirt at all. Nothing. Jamie, are you listening to me?"

I'm too busy scrubbing my shirt to answer her. Soapy water slops over the basin and splashes my bare feet. I don't care. I have to keep working until the shirt is clean—absolutely clean.

Until every trace of blood has disappeared.

I'M LED THROUGH THE MAGIC DOOR and into the unlocked section of the psych unit. I consider breaking away from the nurse at my side and making a run for it, although I know I wouldn't get very far—a seventeen-year-old girl running through the halls in a hospital gown and foam-rubber slippers is bound to be noticed. Besides, where would I go? What do you do when you realize that all of your escape routes are completely blocked off?

"Right on time," Dr. Hackett says, coming down the hall. "In here, Jamie, please." She opens the door to a sunny little office. "I'll give you a call when we're through," she says to the nurse.

I take the chair in front of her desk. I wonder if I look as ratty as I feel. I wish I'd thought to comb my hair. I tuck it behind my ears and smooth out my baggy robe. I don't want to look like an institutionalized mental patient, but of course, that's exactly what I am.

"Let's talk about it," the doctor says, pulling up a chair so we're facing each other. "Let's talk about what happened last night."

I study the ID tag clipped to the pocket of her

white coat: L. HACKETT, M.D., PSYCH SERVICES & CHIEF OF STAFF.

"I forgot you were chief of staff here," I say. "That's kind of an important thing, right? The head of all the doctors?"

She smiles. "Right."

"The nurse was telling my mom you were this fantastic doctor, and my mom . . . it was pathetic, sort of, how relieved my mom got."

"Your mother's scared. She doesn't understand what happened to you last night."

I can feel myself start tensing up. More than a little obvious, with my hands clutching the arms of my chair. I try to relax a little so the doctor won't notice.

"I saw some kids in the park last night," I say. "Kids playing baseball—and when they ran off the field—I don't know, I guess it reminded me of the night I met Webb."

"It set off an episode?"

"You could say that, yeah. I watched him walk farther and farther away from me, and I knew I'd never see him again."

"You know now, don't you?" she asks. "We started to talk about this yesterday. You know where Webb is."

My eyes suddenly sting with tears. "Yes."

"Where?"

"Nowhere. In my heart, maybe, or my head. But not out in the world anywhere."

"Why do you think he came into your life?"

"I don't know. He's been with me so long—ever since I was nine—that I hardly remember a time without him. And this spring we started seeing each other more than ever; we were really becoming close."

"You started spending more and more time with Webb this spring, and your mother didn't notice?"

"She was in Chicago a lot preparing for the trial." I look at her. "I didn't need Webb because my *mommy* neglected me, if that's what you're thinking."

"No, that's not what I'm thinking," the doctor says. "Jamie . . . does your mother know about Webb?"

I shake my head. "I had to keep him a secret from her."

"Why?"

When I shrug and won't answer, the doctor says: "Jamie, do you remember telling me that the Renfro trial isn't the only high-profile trial your mom ever worked on?"

"Sort of . . ."

"There was another famous trial she worked on back when she was a prosecutor, wasn't there?"

"That was a long time ago."

"She prosecuted a child molester, didn't she? That must have been a frightening time for you and your mother. Your mom received some threatening mail, didn't she, and she was concerned for your safety—"

"I don't remember much about that time; just what my mom told me."

"Do you think the Renfro trial—with its disturbing elements and all its publicity, which has demanded so much of your mother's time—do you think maybe it triggered some scary memories of the other trial? Do you think that's why you needed Webb so much this spring?"

"No!" I swallow hard. "Look, Webb's gone. That's what you wanted, isn't it? Why do we have to talk about some other trial my mom worked on?"

"Jamie, Webb came into your life while your mom was working on that other trial, didn't he? He came into your life one night when you were nine years old; one night when you were alone in the park because the baby-sitter didn't pick you up—"

"I don't remember!" I feel like she's leading me somewhere I don't want to go. Someplace I've been careful to avoid for a long, long time. "How come I have to be in the hospital? It was stupid, what I did last night, falling apart like that, but it won't happen again, I *swear* it won't. Can't you just let me go home?"

"No." Her expression makes it clear that it's not up for discussion; not at all. "I don't want you to have to battle the outside world right now," she says. "I think it's going to take all the strength you have to deal with whatever it is you're so afraid of."

"I'm not *afraid* of anything."

The doctor clasps her hands behind her head and looks at me. "Your face reveals more than you think it does."

"God, it's like you're on this incredible power trip where you think you know everything about me! You don't! You don't know me at *all!*"

"Tell me why you're so angry."

"Because you took Webb away from me! Because I woke up in a locked psychiatric ward! Because I want to get the hell out of this office and I *can't!*"

"You can leave if you want," the doctor says, reaching for the phone. "I'll have the nurse take you back to your room; we can talk again tomorrow."

I jump up and go to the door. My hand lingers on the doorknob, but it's like something is holding me back.

"It isn't locked," the doctor says.

"I was talking to Morgan earlier, and she said . . . she said that deep down I know how to get myself out of here."

It's quiet for a moment, then: "Morgan has a special insight into the kind of fear we're talking about; insight I don't have."

"Because of what she went through last winter, you mean? Because of her friend's death?"

"Yes."

"She got better by facing it."

"Yes."

I turn around and look at her. She puts the phone down. "I get these memory flashes," I blurt out. "They're like scenes from a magic show where it's all mirrors and special effects, where any picture that appears in front of my eyes vanishes in a puff of blue smoke before I can get a good look at it. Every time I start to see the scene clearly, something gets in the way and stops me. Something *stops* me."

"Webb stops you," the doctor says.

I just stare at her.

"Webb stops you. He's been protecting you for a long time, Jamie."

I need to sit down. I make it back to the chair just as my knees give out.

"He's gone now, though," I say.

"Yes."

Suddenly I'm pulled into a vortex of memory, sent spinning back to that night in the park when I was nine years old.

"I told you some of it," I hear myself say. "I told you about the night I was all alone on the baseball field."

"The baby-sitter never came to pick you up."

"I waited for her a long time, then I heard something—footsteps in the bushes." I look at her. "I can't remember; it was too long ago."

"Webb isn't here now to stand between you and the memory," the doctor says.

My heart quickens. "It's a place I don't want to go. Don't make me talk about it."

The doctor leans forward. I notice a delicate gold chain dangling from her neck, and I wonder if it was a gift from someone special in her life—a friend, maybe, or a lover. I know so little about her personal life; she knows a frightening amount about mine.

"It's time for you to tell me what happened that night, Jamie," she says. "It's time for you to tell me everything."

✻ PART THREE ✻

31

IT'S LIKE I HAVE DUAL VISION: I CAN SEE
the doctor and the baseball field at the same
time.

"Where are you?" the doctor asks.

"In the park, at the edge of the baseball field,"
I say. "I promised Ellis I'd wait for her by the
bleachers, but she never came."

"Ellis was the baby-sitter."

"Yes." I'm surrounded by the cold fog. "It's like
it's happening now. . . ."

"Help me see it," the doctor says. "Take me
with you."

"It's nighttime," I say, the park slowly coming to
life around me, the doctor fading off into the background somewhere. "It's nighttime, and I'm all
alone. . . ."

I hear footsteps in the woods; the sound of dry
leaves crunching underfoot. I see a flash of something in the bushes—a man in a hooded red sweatshirt and sunglasses. The sunglasses scare me more
than anything; no one wears sunglasses at night.
He approaches me so quickly the only thing I can
think to do is reach down and grab a stick—a

weapon to protect myself—but he pulls it out of my hand and snaps it in two.

"Shouldn't play with sticks, Jamie," he says, tossing the broken pieces to the ground. "You might hurt yourself."

He knows me. Somehow he knows me, but I've never seen him before.

"Look at you! You look just like a scared little rabbit." He holds his hand out. "You come with me, darlin'."

I can't move. I'm paralyzed.

"Did you hear what I said?" he asks, reaching for me. "Come on, I'm not going to hurt you."

I back away from him.

"Get over here," he says, and I turn and try to run, but he grabs my hand. "No, no, no, I'm afraid you'll have to come with me. We're going for a little ride."

I open my mouth, but suddenly there's no air in my lungs—I can't yell or scream or make any sound at all.

"I've been planning this for a long time, Jamie," he says, pulling me into the bushes. When I stumble, he jerks me to my feet like I'm a rag doll. "Your mother won't know you're missing for quite a while," he says, "not with those long hours she's been keeping down at the courthouse. I know lots about your mother, Jamie. You'd be surprised, the things I know."

He pulls me into a clearing, where I can see a

big old sedan parked off in the distance on a dirt road.

"There it is," he says. "The Jamie-mobile." He scoops me up and carries me to the car. "You're light as feathers," he says, throwing me across to the passenger side and then jumping into the driver's seat. He whips his sunglasses off, pulls the hood back on his sweatshirt. I can see his face in the moonlight; a young face, a face full of hatred. "Go ahead. Take a good look. Doesn't matter. You won't be telling anyone about me."

"No, I won't tell anyone," I whisper. "I won't tell, I promise."

"Shut up." He turns a key in the ignition, and suddenly I'm thrown back against the seat as he tears down the bumpy dirt road.

"You can thank your mother for this little trip we're taking, Jamie," the stranger says. "She's a bad person, did you know that?"

I'm thinking: This has something to do with my mom. I know my mom isn't a bad person, but this man thinks she is.

"What right does your mother have to play God, Jamie? To decide who goes free and who doesn't?"

The fear suddenly explodes inside me. "The baby-sitter will tell my mom! She'll tell my mom I wasn't in the park!"

"God, you're dumb."

I wonder if he's hurt Ellis. I wonder where she is.

"Your mother's destroying my family, Jamie," the stranger says. "Now I'm going to destroy hers."

I sit very still. I don't want to make this person any angrier than he is.

"I've seen some of the trial on TV. Your mother struts around preening for the camera and tells the whole world how twisted my brother is. It's cost us big time, Jamie, all of us—my mother and father and me. We get hate mail and sick phone calls. The phone calls are the worst. The things people say about my brother! *Terrible* things. Vicious things. Do you think that's right?"

We're going too fast for me to jump out of the car. Even if I had a chance to escape, how would I get away from him? Where would I go? We're out in the country, and the landscape is dark and deserted—I don't see any houses or cars or people anywhere.

"I think your mother's finished with this trial, Jamie," the stranger says. "I have a feeling she's going to be too upset to go down to the courthouse tomorrow."

The car swerves sharply onto a gravel road. There's a building off in distance. I can see blue light shining in the window.

"Maybe I made it up," I say. I'm back in the doctor's office now. I wait. I hope so much she'll agree with me. "I could have done that, right? Kids are supposed to have wild imaginations, aren't they? Maybe I made the whole thing up."

"No," the doctor says. Her eyes are troubled. It would be so much easier for me if she were one of those impassive shrinks who never showed any emotion. "I don't think this is something you made up," she says. "Where is the stranger taking you?"

"To a little gas station out in the middle of nowhere."

"He takes you to a gas station? Is anyone there?"

"No, it's closed, I guess, but he has a key to the office. He drags me inside. . . ."

The office is tiny with a dirty checkerboard floor. Blue light from a neon sign in the window spells something backward across the stranger's chest.

"Like where I work, Jamie?" he asks. "The owner couldn't get along without me. I practically run the place. I even stopped a robbery last year. Know what I did? Pretended I was opening the cash register, but I was really reaching for the owner's gun. I held it on him till the police showed up. Everyone called me a hero."

The stranger picks up the telephone, an old-fashioned rotary phone that goes *clickety-clickety-click* as he dials.

"I did it," he says into the phone. "It went off just like we planned. You better hurry."

He hangs up. I wedge myself into a little corner next to the cash register. It's as far away from him as I can get.

He looks at me and laughs. "Playing hide-and-seek? It's my favorite game. I've been playing it with the police for weeks now, only they don't know I'm the one they're looking for. Did you know you've been under police protection, Jamie? They've been watching you ever since I sent some letters to your mother. They watch you all the time when you're out in public. Too bad no one told them you were playing baseball tonight, huh? Too bad that baby-sitter never made it to the park to fetch you."

He comes over to me and twirls some of my hair around his finger. He can reach me, even though I'm in that narrow little space. "You're not going anywhere; you might as well make up your mind. . . ."

"I can't keep talking about this!" I hear myself saying to the doctor. "Dr. Hackett, please, it's like I'm *there*! It's like it's happening all over again! I can't talk about this anymore!"

"Yes, you can," the doctor says. She's the only one I have now, the only one who can lead me out of the darkness, bring me back here where it's safe, but she won't do it—I can see she's not going to do it. "I want you to keep going, Jamie. Tell me what's happening." And she sends me back to that night, back to the stranger.

❋ ❋ ❋

"Your mother thinks she's so smart," he whispers, "but looks like I'm smarter, doesn't it? I got you here, right where I want you, and she doesn't even have a clue."

He lights a cigarette and squints at me.

"You know what's going to happen, don't you?" he asks. "Sure you do. Go ahead and cry. Won't change anything. Won't change a damn thing."

The sound of a car in the distance distracts him, and he looks out the window. He's not in any hurry, though. He walks over to the phone and rips the cord out of the wall. "Don't you go anywhere. I'll be right back."

The stranger steps outside and smokes his cigarette and watches the gravel road. Someone is coming. The person he called is coming. What will happen to me when there are two of them?

"What are you doing while the stranger is outside?" the doctor asks.

"Looking around for another way out," I say. "There isn't one. I stay where I am, in that tight little corner next to the cash register. It's so quiet, except for the neon sign making this electric *zzzt-zzzt-zzzt* sound. The blue letters in the sign are backward, but I can read them. I wonder if they spell out the name of the owner. I hope he'll come back for some reason and discover what's going on.

I hope he'll rescue me. That's all I can think about: There's the name of the person who will come rescue me."

"What does the neon sign spell?"

I put my head in my hands. "I think it's supposed to be Webber's, but the last few letters are burnt out."

I look up at the doctor. She sees it, too, but waits for me to say it: "The last few letters are burnt out . . . the sign spells Webb! It spells *Webb!*"

A car jerks to a stop in front of the gas station. The stranger tosses his cigarette down and walks to the driver's side of the car.

I recognize the car.

I recognize the driver.

Ellis.

"Ellis knows the stranger?" the doctor asks.

"It's like she can't wait to jump into his arms. He whirls her around, and as they get closer to the office I can hear her—God, she's laughing like this is some kind of *party!*" I'm holding on to the arms of my chair so tightly that my fingers are numb. "She was supposed to be my *friend*! I trusted her!"

"Hey, Jamie," the stranger says, "meet my girlfriend, Ellis. Oh, I'm sorry, I forgot! You already know her!"

Ellis sees me. Her face turns white. "Jackson, come on, what *is* this?"

"What is this? Why, this is your little *friend,* Ellis."

"Jackson, I thought you were going to take her right to the cabin! She's not supposed to know I'm connected to this in any way!"

"I know we talked about taking her to my cabin," the stranger says, "but I've had something else in mind all along. Something I couldn't tell you about till now."

Ellis pulls away from him. "We had a deal. A kidnapping, so we could get enough money to go away together! No one would know I helped you. No one would *know.*"

"I don't care how much money Jamie's mother has, Ellis. This isn't about money."

"Then *why?* What's the point if we aren't doing this for money? What's the *point!*"

"What's the point?" The stranger looks at me. "Tell her, Jamie. Tell her what the point is."

When I don't answer, when I can't speak, he puts his hand under my chin and says in a quiet voice: "Did you *hear* me? Tell her what the point is."

"He wants to hurt my *mom!*" I scream. "He wants to hurt *me!*"

The stranger nods. "Very good, Jamie." He turns to Ellis. "I could have gone after the mother, but this is better, don't you think? Her mother will never forget what happens tonight. By tomorrow she'll have to drop out of the trial. By tomorrow she'll know what it's like to have her life destroyed—"

"What are you *talking* about?" Ellis shrieks. "What does the trial have to do with *you*? Why do you care whether or not Jamie's mother prosecutes some pervert who goes after little children—"

It's awful, what happens next: The stranger cracks Ellis across the face. I don't want to look, but I'm afraid not to. I have to be prepared to protect myself.

"That's my brother you're talking about, Ellis," the stranger says calmly.

Ellis looks stunned. She puts her hand to her face. "Jackson, no—"

"By the way, Jackson Farrell isn't my real name—I got that one out of the phone book. I'm really Harlan White. Sorry I had to lie, Ellis, but I couldn't take a chance on you knowing my real name and making a connection to the case Jamie's mom is prosecuting. That could've made things a bit difficult for me, don't you think?"

"No, please, you said no one would get hurt—"

"*No, please,*" he mocks. "What did you think would happen to Jamie? Tell me. I really want to know."

"You promised . . . you promised you'd just keep her at the cabin for a day or two—you said nothing would happen to her!"

"You're pitiful, Ellis. Pitiful. You think it was

just an *accident* that I happened into your life when I did?"

Ellis slowly edges away from him. "Don't . . . I don't want to hear this—"

"My brother showed me a picture from the local paper," he says. "A picture of Jamie and her mother at a Girl Scout meeting. I remember the caption: 'Deputy DA Speaks at Career Day.' I found out where the scouts met, but I could never get close enough to Jamie to do anything. There were always too many people around when the kids left the building: the parents or troop leaders or you. I decided you were the easiest way to get to Jamie."

The stranger comes toward me. I hold my breath, but he's not reaching for me. His hand disappears under the cash register. He pulls out a gun.

"I learned your whole routine, Ellis. I knew you picked Jamie up every Tuesday after scouts. You always got out of the car and visited with some of the other moms and dads who were waiting for their kids. I walked by you one day and heard you complaining to a woman about your social life—or lack of one, I should say. I figured it'd be easy to bump into you the next day and charm you a bit—and I did, didn't I? That meeting led to another between us, and another, and another . . ."

"Please," Ellis says. She backs away from the stranger and secretly nudges me with her hand. I grab her shaking fingers. "*Please . . .*"

"You're no better than I am, Ellis," the stranger says. "You're the one who took Jamie to her baseball game tonight, even though her mother told you not to. You're the one who left her alone in the park, knowing what was going to happen to her."

"But I didn't know you wanted to—to—" She stops abruptly, then says quietly, "You sent those letters to Jamie's mom, didn't you? You sent those threats."

"Too bad it took you so long to figure it out," the stranger says. "You ladies are going on a little ride with old Harlan. Come along, Ellis. Bring our friend."

Ellis leads me forward a few steps, then suddenly she shoves me toward the door. *"Jamie, run!"* she screams. *"Run!"*

I twist the hem of my hospital gown and look at the doctor. "I shouldn't have told you so much," I say. "I want to go back to my room."

"What happened after Ellis shoved you toward the door?"

"The stranger tried to hurt her, but she fought with him. The gun flew out of his hand."

"What did you do?"

"Tried to get out. I tried to get out, but the door was stuck; I couldn't get it open."

"What happened next?"

"I heard a noise."

"What kind of noise?"

"A firecracker. I heard a firecracker explode."

"It wasn't really a firecracker, though, was it?"

"No."

"What made the noise?"

"I don't know."

"Was it the gun?"

"I want to go back to my room."

"Jamie." She takes my hands. Hers are so warm. "Did someone fire the gun?"

"Yes."

"Who?"

"I don't know."

"Try to see it. Is the stranger holding the gun?"

"No."

"Ellis?"

"No."

"Who, then?"

Like ice cracking off from a glacier, the memory breaks free. I can see it. All of it.

"I am," I say, grasping her hands as tightly as I can. "I'm holding the gun."

It happens with lightning speed: I point the gun and it fires, throwing me back against the door. I'm not sure what's happened at first, then I see the stranger collapsed on the floor; his shirt soaked in blood.

I can't take my eyes off him.

"Jamie," Ellis says, her voice rising in panic,

"we have to get out of here—we have to get out!"

The gun is at my feet. I don't remember dropping it. Ellis picks it up and shoves me aside so she can get the door open. "Jamie, come on, we have to get out of here!" She yanks the door open. "Jamie, *come on*!"

I'm too frozen to move. Ellis grabs my hand and pulls me outside. We run to the car, and I just stand there while she jumps inside. "Jamie, get in the car!" she yells. "Do what I say! Get *inside*!"

I climb into the car and barely have time to shut the door before her foot slams down on the accelerator and we take off, spraying gravel up around the windows as we peel off into the darkness.

"Jamie, it wasn't supposed to be like this at *all!*" she says, starting to cry. "I never thought—he was going to send for me after he got the money! We were going to have a life together! Jamie, what was I supposed to *do*? I loved him!"

I look over at her. "You have blood on your shirt, Ellis."

She glances down at the blood, black as ink in this pale moonlight. "I never thought anything like this would happen!" she says. "I was going to tell your mom you begged me to take you to the park tonight. I was going to tell her I was sure it'd be safe to leave you there for an hour or two because there were so many other kids around!"

I'm not part of this. Wherever we're heading, I know that I'll meet up with someone soon—someone who will make everything all right. Someone who will protect and take care of me.

"God, what are we going to *do*!" Ellis says. I wonder if she can see to drive; she's crying so hard. "Jamie, you can't tell anyone what happened tonight. Not your mother, not *anyone*. I'll get in trouble if you tell. So will you. Do you understand?"

"Yes," I say.

"Promise you'll never tell."

"Ellis, I want to go home."

Ellis jerks the car to a stop and grabs my arms. "Promise you'll never *tell!*" she screams. "Promise!"

"I promise!"

She lets go of me, and we start down the road again. "I never wanted you to get hurt, Jamie, but it'll happen—I *swear* it will—if you ever tell anyone what happened tonight."

"I won't, Ellis! I promise I'll never tell!"

Ellis is going to kill us, the way she's rocketing through the dark countryside. Eventually she slows down and stops the car on a narrow bridge and tosses the gun over the guardrail. I picture the gun sinking slowly to the bottom of the river. No one will ever find it there.

"I'm going to take you back to the baseball field," Ellis says. "It's the only way, Jamie. Your mother's probably on her way home right now— what if we get to the house just as she does? I can't let her see me like this, not with all this blood on my shirt."

"How will you get the blood out of your shirt, Ellis?"

"Jamie, *listen* to me! I'm going to take you back to the park and as soon as I get home, I'll call your mother. I'll tell her—I'll tell her my car broke down somewhere out in the country and I couldn't pick you up. I'll tell her someone's letting me call from their house while I wait for a tow truck."

"Ellis took you back to the baseball field?" the doctor asks.

"She dropped me off just like she did when I had a game. I started to cry because I was so scared, then he stepped out of the woods and I knew everything would be all right. He was a blond boy, a boy big enough and smart enough to protect me."

The doctor nods. She knows who I mean. I close my eyes and remember what it was like, that first time we met.

Nothing to be frightened of, Jamie, he said. You're not alone anymore. I'm here now; I I look after you. My name s Webb.

32

FOR THE NEXT THREE NIGHTS, TERRIFYING pictures flash through my head when I try to sleep: images of being dragged off the baseball field and of the gun exploding.

Images of blood spattering Ellis's shirt.

"It will take a long time for the pictures to fade," the doctor says at one of my sessions. "This is all brand-new to you, even though it happened eight years ago."

I feel sleep-starved and hollow inside.

"My mom will have to call the police. I did something terrible. She'll have to report it."

"I imagine so." The doctor comes over to the chair I'm sitting in. She crouches down like grown-ups do when they want to be eye-level with little kids. "You're not the one responsible for what happened, Jamie."

"I wish I could just escape into the world I shared with Webb," I say. "Nothing bad ever happened to me there."

"Nothing happened there at all, did it? Not really."

"It was my sanctuary."

"It was your prison."

I look at her. "How am I supposed to handle this without him?"

"You won't have to handle it on your own."

"My mom, you mean?"

"Yes." She goes over to her chair. "This might be a good time to talk about your mom. She called me earlier; she's anxious to come see you."

Electricity shoots through my body. "No. I'm not ready."

"Jamie, it will help you if you can tell her what happened that night."

I bite the corner of my thumbnail. "No. Not yet."

"What if I call her and ask her to come tomorrow after court adjourns for the day?"

I shake my head.

The doctor waits. She knows me by now. Sometimes things sink into my brain in these quiet little pauses when we're not talking.

"If I talk to my mom," I say, "if I tell her what happened, do you think it'll really help me? Will it stop those creepy pictures that keep flashing through my head?"

"It'll be a first step toward stopping them."

"You'll be here when I tell her?" I ask.

"Yes."

"Okay," I say, after a minute.

"Good. We'll ask her to come tomorrow, then."

I'm not sure how she does it, exactly: how she nudges me someplace I never thought I'd be able to go. Maybe she really does have a magic wand stashed around here someplace.

That afternoon I'm sitting alone in the TV room watching some of the trial. It's awful, how pale and drawn my mom looks, but that shouldn't surprise me, not after what I've put her through. It's only going to get worse, I think, after I tell her my secret.

"Jamie? Hi." I turn to see Morgan coming into the room. "The nurses said you were in here."

"Yeah, I'm watching some of the trial."

She holds up a pair of bright red socks with sparkly threads woven through them. "I looked all over the city, Jamie, and this is as close as I could come to ruby slippers." She drops the socks into my lap.

I laugh. "Thanks. Let's see if they work." I kick off my ugly foam rubber slippers and pull on the red socks. I click my heels together three times. "They seem to be defective. I'm still here."

"Damn," Morgan says. "I guess I'll have to take them back to the store and get a refund."

"No, I want to keep them, even if they don't have magical powers."

She sits down next to me. "You look good."

"Oh, right," I say, making a face. "No hair dryer, no makeup, and wow—look at this designer hospital wardrobe. I'm a regular supermodel."

"Bet you can't wait to get out of here, right?"

"I felt that way a few days ago, but not now. I

don't even want to *think* about leaving here and having to deal with the world on my own, without . . ." I look at her. "It's a long story. I'll tell you about it sometime, Morgan, but not now, okay?"

"You don't have to tell me anything. You don't have to talk at all if you don't want to."

"Thanks. I've been talking about myself ever since I got here, it seems. I think I'm all talked out."

"Mind if I just sit here with you and watch some of the trial?"

"No, I'd like that."

She never made me feel like I was weird or a head case. She never laughed at me like the weasels did back home. She made sure I got help when I needed it, she always said the right things to me, she came here just to hang out with me—and she brought me a pair of ruby slippers. Well, sort of. I look down at my sparkly fake-ruby-slipper-socks and wiggle my toes. Morgan notices and laughs. I feel a lightness in my chest, the first buoyant feeling I've had since I've been here.

So this is what it's like to have a friend, I think.

This is what it's like.

33

"TAKE SOME DEEP BREATHS," THE DOCTOR
says, and I do, and it doesn't help.

I'm sitting in her office while we wait for my
mom. I've done everything I can so my mom won't
think I look like a refugee from the psych ward:
I've made sure my hair is combed and I've ditched
the hospital haute couture and am wearing the
same shirt and jeans I wore the night I flipped out
in the ER. I can't believe I actually thought there
was blood on this shirt—that makes me realize
what a truly demented state I was in. I'm just hoping I don't slip back into Psycholand when I tell my
mom the secret I've been keeping all these years.

"I'm not sure I'm brave enough for this," I say. "I
wish I could just run to Webb, like I always have."

"Webb existed to protect you from a secret,"
the doctor says. "You have someone else to run to
now." And she looks over to the doorway, where
my mother stands.

It takes a long time before I can start telling my
mother about that night. We talk first of little
things: about the overnight bag she's brought that
contains a change of clothes for me. About whether

or not she should bring another pair of jeans. Another sweater, maybe.

"I don't think Jamie will need anything else," the doctor says. "I'm hoping to release her from the hospital in the next day or two."

"So soon?" my mother asks. She sounds so hopeful. "Things are going well, then?"

The question is directed at the doctor, but the doctor waits for me to answer it.

"Mom," I say, after a long moment. "Mom, something happened to me a long time ago. Something happened that night Ellis forgot to pick me up from my baseball game."

My mother doesn't get it at first, then her eyes widen with fear.

"Mom, I hate to give you more to worry about while the Renfro trial is going on—"

"I don't give a damn about the Renfro trial," my mother says, her voice catching. "*You're* what's important. Tell me what happened."

I paint the picture slowly, starting with the stranger who dragged me off the baseball field and into his car. When I get to the part about being forced into Webber's gas station, all the color drains from my mother's face.

"Some stranger took you to *Webber's*?" she asks, panic in her voice. "Jamie, what was the name of the man who took you there? What was his *name*?"

"Harlan. Harlan White. Mom, please, it scares me to see you so frightened!"

"Harlan White was the brother of the man I prosecuted," my mother says bluntly, looking at me with such intensity I can hardly stand it. "Did he *hurt* you? Did he *do* anything to you?"

I get up out of my chair and walk over to the window so I don't have to see my mother or the doctor. It's easier when I don't have to look into their eyes. "No! He didn't touch me. Not in the way you mean. Mom, he was Ellis's boyfriend. They planned the kidnapping together."

I don't have to see my mother to know her reaction. I can hear her breath quicken. She's softly saying, "No . . ."

"Ellis didn't know Harlan was the brother of the man you were prosecuting," I say. "He tricked her, Mom. It was supposed to be a kidnapping for money. She loved him so much she agreed to help him, but when she got to the gas station she found out the truth: that Harlan wanted to hurt me. He wanted to hurt her, too."

"Jamie," my mother says weakly, "Harlan White was shot and killed that night. The police never found out who did it. They never found the weapon. Did Ellis . . . did she . . ."

"They were fighting," I hear myself say. "I was afraid he was going to hurt Ellis so I picked up the gun."

I turn around and look at my mother.

"The gun went off, Mom. It went off and killed Harlan."

Her face is frozen in disbelief. For a moment I think this is the worst punishment I could get—I've stunned my mother so much she can't even react at all.

"Mom, say something!" I can't hold it together any longer. I'm sobbing and trying to talk at the same time: "Please *say* something!"

My mother jumps up from her chair and comes over and puts her arms around me. "It's all right," she says. "It's all right now."

"Ellis said I'd get into trouble if I told! On the way back to the baseball field she threw the gun in the river. She made me promise to keep it all a secret, but she didn't have to worry; I didn't remember *any* of it. I didn't *want* to remember."

"When I picked you up at the baseball field that night, you were so quiet. *Too* quiet. Like you were off in your own world—"

"I was," I say. "Ever since that night I've lived in two worlds: the world I walk around in and go to school in, and a fantasy world where nothing bad ever happens to me, where I created a friend named Webb who's protected me from the secret all this time."

The warmth of her body makes me feel quieter inside. I'm aware of the doctor stepping out into the hall so my mother and I can be alone. "Harlan wrote those threatening letters you got, Mom. He kept bragging about how you wouldn't be able to finish the trial if something happened to me."

"You've kept this locked inside all these years?" my mother asks. "Honey, I'm sorry. I'm so *sorry!*"

"Mom? What will happen to me now? Will I get into trouble?"

"No! You were nine years old! You saved your *life* that night! Ellis's, too! No, you won't get into trouble."

"What about Ellis?"

"Ellis is another story. She's an accessory to kidnapping."

She hugs me even tighter. I am so calm inside, just like when I was with Webb.

"I always worried that you lived too much in your own world," my mother says. "I wish I'd known just *how* real it was to you and why you were there."

I close my eyes and call Webb, but the beach we used to walk on is deserted now. There's no sign of my friend. No indication that he was ever here. I watch as the world we once shared slowly evaporates into a fine white mist.

* PART FOUR *

34

"I THINK," THE DOCTOR SAYS, "THAT I'M the one doing all the work today."

I've never seen her angry, never seen her lose her cool, but there's no missing the "Playtime is over" tone in her voice.

"I just don't feel like it," I say. "I'm tired of answering questions and going over everything that's happened."

I've been out of the hospital for a few days, and this is my first time back here in the doctor's downtown office. I keep watching the clock on her desk, counting the seconds till this session is over.

She turns the clock around so I can't see it. "Jamie, I can't help you if you won't talk to me—"

"Talking only makes me feel worse."

"You felt better for a while, didn't you? After you told your mom about what happened."

"For a while, maybe. But not now. All of a sudden there's this—I don't know—just this cold sort of emptiness inside. Talking isn't going to change that."

"You're grieving," the doctor says.

I look at her. "Grieving . . . for what?"

"Someone you care deeply about isn't here anymore."

"Webb, you mean?"

"Yes."

"You make it sound like I'm in mourning or something."

"You are."

I can feel my face getting hot. "You don't think it's weird for me to miss him?"

"You lived through a night of terror when you were nine, and Webb was the only one who knew about it. He protected you, looked out for you. Why wouldn't you miss him?"

I clear my throat. "Sometimes . . . sometimes I'll close my eyes and try to remember what he looked like—what he sounded like—and I *can't*. I can't remember, and it bothers me."

"I know," she says quietly. "But it's just another sign you've let him go. You're disengaging from the world you shared with him."

"I was happier there."

"Jamie."

"I *was*."

"The real world also has some good things to offer," the doctor says.

"I don't care about the real world."

"You won't always feel this way." She sounds so sure of what she's saying. I wish I could believe her. I *want* to believe her. "You've spent almost half of your life with Webb, and it's going to take a while before you get used to living here without him," she says. "It's going to take time, and it's not going to be easy."

✳   ✳   ✳

She's right about that: It's harder than I'd thought, facing the world without him. My way of coping is to basically sentence myself to house arrest unless I have to go out for a doctor's appointment. I've even put my friendship with Morgan on hold. I've hardly spoken to her when I've seen her at the doctor's office, and she backed off, sort of, when I told her I wasn't up to doing anything yet. Today, though, she kept calling and talking to the machine:

"Come on, Jamie, pick up . . . I know you're there. What—do I have to come over there just so I can talk to you?"

She called ten times. I got so tired of hearing the phone ring that I finally ended up rewarding her persistence: "Morgan?"

"Jamie, hi . . . what are you doing?"

"I'm sitting on the couch wrapped up in a blanket."

"You've been home for over a week. Let's go out for lunch or something."

"I don't feel like it."

"I'm coming over."

"I won't let you in."

"Yes, you will."

Click.

How annoying, I think, as I get dressed. I mean, shouldn't a friend—a real friend—let me hibernate if I want to? I could refuse to let her come up, I guess, but she'd just start calling again. *God . . .*

"If we don't go out," she says, when I let her in, "I'll be forced to make lunch. And you know what a lousy cook I am."

I just look at her. "Why are you doing this to me?"

"It's called friendship."

"You want to know what *I* call it?"

"Not really. Come on, will you? I'm starving."

We eat at a crowded little deli that's overflowing with businesspeople on their lunch breaks.

"Not the fanciest place, maybe," Morgan says, "but their sandwiches are the best." She pops the tab on her can of Diet Coke. "So am I forgiven?"

"For being so bossy, you mean?" I ask. "Yeah. I guess I needed a kick-start of some kind—I've been hibernating ever since I got home from the hospital."

"I know what it's like to want to hide in a blanket."

I pick up my turkey on rye, but I can't eat it. I push it aside. "I want to tell you why I was in the hospital, Morgan, okay? I mean, I *need* to tell you."

She looks at me, all serious and everything. "If you're sure you want to—"

"I'm sure," I say, and I start telling her about the night I was taken off the baseball field, about the stranger and the baby-sitter. When I get to the part about the gun exploding, her eyes fill with tears. I hand her a skinny paper napkin.

"I was so terrified that night that I—well, I created someone to protect me," I say, "and that's where Webb comes in."

She looks at me, stunned. "What do you mean? He's not . . ."

I nod. "Pretty sick, huh?"

She wipes her eyes. "No, I didn't mean that. Just . . . he sounded so wonderful, and . . ." She looks at me. "He's gone now?"

"Yeah."

"I can't believe you lived through something so horrible," she says. "You won't have to . . . you won't get into trouble, will you? You were so young when it happened."

"My mom says it's a clear-cut case of self-defense, but I'll still have to fly back to California one of these days and tell the police what happened. I'm just not ready to do it yet. I need time to adjust to everything."

"Yeah, I can imagine."

"I was afraid to tell you," I say. "Afraid of what you'd think."

"Jamie, come on, you never have to worry about what I think."

"Thanks, but I've kept the secret for so many years—even from myself—that it's hard to talk about."

"How are you managing without him?"

"I'm not," I say.

She's quiet a minute. Then she looks at me and says, "The night my best friend was killed, I went sort of crazy. My aunt had to give me a shot of Valium because I was shaking so hard—that's what bad shape I was in. But as devastating as that night was, it wasn't anything compared to what came afterward: carving out a life without him."

"That's where I am now."

"I had good days and bad," she says. "More good, eventually, than bad."

I look at her. "Really?"

"Yeah," she says. "Really. You just have to hang in there till things gets better."

We finish lunch and walk back to my apartment. It's sunny and windy, and we hustle across the street with a crowd of pedestrians against the blinking DON'T WALK sign. It's just sort of nice to have a friend at my side who cared enough about me to drag me out into the sunshine—makes me realize that I'm not as alone as I thought I was, that I'm not, at least for the moment, on the outside looking in.

35

MOM SPENDS AN HOUR ON THE PHONE THAT
night talking with her law partner back in California about my "case." When she hangs up, she
shows me a legal pad filled with her notes. "I'm trying to get a jump on organizing some of the information we'll need when we go back home and talk
to the authorities." She tucks the legal pad into her
briefcase.

"I'm not ready to even think about it."

"No, not yet, darling," she says quickly. "Of
course not. I suppose I just feel better if I can at
least start doing something about that terrible
ordeal you went through."

The phone rings. If tonight's like most nights, this
is just the first of five—six—seven calls she'll get from
her colleagues about the Renfro trial. I'm beginning to
think of Sally Renfro as my unofficial sister.

Maybe my mom should adopt her.

The doctor sits, her fingers curled around a cup
of coffee, and listens while I fill her in on some of
the things that have happened in the last few days.

"My mom's really incredible," I say. "She spends
something like ten hours at the courthouse every

day, then at night, when she's not discussing the trial with her friends, she's on the phone with her law partner back in California. He's going to be my attorney and guide us through the legal maze once I'm ready to go back home and give my statement to the police. My mom's even made up a file for me with all these notes in it."

The doctor doesn't say anything at first. I can't stand the way she studies me. She listens too hard. She hears things I haven't told her.

"You're so calm when you talk about your mother," she says.

I'm just sort of shocked at that. "Why shouldn't I be calm?"

"Something terrible happened to you when you were nine years old, and you couldn't even share it with her."

"That wasn't my mom's fault."

"No, it wasn't her fault."

"She didn't know what was happening that night," I say. "She didn't know some stranger dragged me off the baseball field, she didn't know where he took me, what he tried to do to me, what I ended up doing." A sudden flash of rage hits me. "She didn't have a *clue*!" I sit there, horrified, and look at the doctor. "I didn't mean to make it sound like I blame my mom. I don't. She's not the one who hurt me, the one who . . . I'm mad at Ellis and the stranger, not at my mom."

"A nine-year-old might not be as reasonable as

you are, though," the doctor says. "A nine-year-old might be filled with a lot of anger."

"I'm not angry at my mom. I told you. And I'm not nine anymore. Why do we have to keep talking about this?"

"I think you lost something important the night you were taken off the baseball field," the doctor says. "I just want to help you reclaim it."

I get up and pace around the office a bit and look out the window. "Did you know the secret about Webb right from the start?" I ask. "Did you know it the first time you saw me in the emergency room?"

"Yes," she says.

"You never made me feel like I was crazy, though."

"You weren't crazy. You created a way to survive."

I turn around and look at her. "I wish I could just deal with the same stuff everyone else my age is dealing with. You know: like worrying about finishing some stupid term paper or hoping I can find the perfect dress for the prom. I guess I just want"—my voice breaks—"I want a normal life like that."

"You'll get there," the doctor says. "I'm so sure about you, Jamie. Nothing's going to stop you from having the life you want."

"I used to feel that anything was possible when I was with him. With Webb. And I sort of feel that way here—when I'm talking to you—like maybe things will get better."

"You feel hopeful."

"Hopeful, yeah. I'm afraid it'll disappear when I walk out of here. I'm afraid it won't last."

"No," the doctor says firmly. "It's not going to disappear. It's just a glimmer of some of the good that's ahead. A preview of things to come."

36

"OKAY, HERE'S A QUESTION FOR YOU," I whisper to Morgan. "That guy over there in the blue T-shirt wants to buy me a frappuccino. What do I do?"

We're at Juice 'n' Java, Morgan and I. She's sipping a caffe latte at our table, and I've just returned from the counter where I had a split-second conversation with a very cute guy standing next to me:

"The raspberry mocha-chip frappuccino is really good," he said. "Would you like to join me? My treat."

"Oh," I said. "Oh . . . well, I'm here with a friend—just a minute. Let me talk to her and—just a minute."

God, I sounded completely idiotic. So here I am, back at the table, telling Morgan what he's just asked me.

"He's tall, cute, and he has a quirky smile," she says. "Jamie, do I *really* have to tell you what to do?"

"I don't even know him, though."

She squints across the room. "He's wearing an Art Institute of Chicago T-shirt and it's got paint on it. Jamie, he's an art student. He's cute. What are you waiting for?"

"God, I'm such a *moron* when it comes to things like this," I say. "I've been so busy the last few years just trying to keep my sanity that I have absolutely no social skills."

"So you're a late bloomer. So what? You'll have fun making up for lost time."

"Well, what about you? We were supposed to have coffee together."

"Jamie, do you see how *cute* he is? Go over there and let him buy you your frappuccino. Go on. I'll sit here like an Olympic judge and score your first coffee date. If you do really well, I'll hold up a card with a nine point nine on it for technical ability—"

"Oh, please . . ."

He tells me his name, but I don't really hear it. He tells me what he's studying, but it doesn't sink in. I do a lot of nodding. I try to fake being a normal person. He listens to me talk, and I listen to him. I drink my frappuccino, even though I'm way too nervous to enjoy it. I try to smile.

I'm sure Morgan will hold up a score card any second that has a minus ten on it.

But before he leaves, he scribbles something down on a Juice 'n' Java napkin and hands it to me.

His phone number.

"Well, well," Morgan says later. "He gave you his phone number? Your technical ability definitely rates a nine point nine. Maybe even a ten."

"Cut it out!"

"Are you going to call him?"

"Hey, give me a break. I'm just sort of waking up to the real world here. I need a little time."

"I go into Juice 'n' Java almost every day and no guy's *ever* offered to buy me coffee."

"I guess I just have that special something every man is searching for," I say. "A kind of fresh-scrubbed 'I just got out of the psychiatric ward and I'm really confused' look that's really irresistible."

"Not funny!" Morgan says, but we both end up laughing.

On the way home, Morgan points out a dance school across the street. "That's where my friend Jimmy studied," she says. "He was so talented. I'm sure he would have ended up on Broadway someday and . . ." I think maybe she's going to cry, but she pulls herself together. "Sorry. I never know when it's going to hit."

"You don't have to apologize for anything," I say. "You've seen me at my worst, remember?"

"I know."

"What do you miss most about him?"

"Oh," she says, "I miss the verbal shorthand between us."

"You're lucky. I've never had that with a friend."

"Are you kidding? We come pretty close, don't we?"

"Yeah, I guess we do." We start walking again. "Hey, promise you'll come visit when my mom and I go back to California. I'd love to take you to Otter Cove. It's such a cool, surreal place."

"Otter Cove? With actual otters, you mean?"

I look at her. "Yes, they tried using fake ones, but somehow it just didn't go over too well with the tourists."

"Otters," she muses. "They swim in the water, right?"

"Right."

"They don't attack, do they?"

"Wow, you really *are* a city girl, aren't you?"

"Yes," she says. "Just think of me as an urban princess."

37

MY MOM'S TWENTY MINUTES LATE, BUT I
don't really care. I'm sitting here at Pasta Mia's,
sipping my Diet Coke and people-watching. The
place is filled with young couples gazing at each
other over the lighted candles, but there are families here, too, laughing and talking, some trying to
quiet their fussy children. I'm the only one here
alone, but I don't feel lonely; maybe it's a carry-
over effect from the fun I had with Morgan this
afternoon and my coffee-date person.

"Sorry I'm late," my mom says, sitting down.
"Have you been waiting long?"

"To see you? Just a couple of days."

"Okay, I deserve that," she says, smiling. "You
get that rapier wit from your father."

"I think I remember him laughing a lot . . .
clowning around . . ."

"Yes. He was so funny. He'd come home from
playing football in the park with his buddies and
have you in hysterics by acting out the whole
game."

Something familiar clicks in my brain. "He used
to come home with lots of scrapes and scratches."

My mom nods, surprised. "You remember that?"

"Did he have a zigzag-shaped scar on his forearm?"

"Yes!"

"It's funny . . . I can see that scar so clearly. I always thought Webb had a scar like that, but I guess I remembered it from Dad. You said he used to take me to the park, didn't you? And Otter Cove."

"Yes. The beach, too. You loved to hold his hand and kick through the purple ice plant along the bay."

"All those things I thought I did with Webb, I did with Dad. Remember the story you told me about Dad backpacking through Europe? I must have remembered hearing that a long time ago, because I made that part of Webb's life, too."

"It's so heartbreaking you lost yourself in some fantasy world because of what happened," my mom says. "If I only could have done something . . . well, we're getting ready to do something now. Which reminds me . . ." She digs in her briefcase until she finds a piece of paper. "I got this fax a little while ago from one of the researchers at the law firm back home." She hands me a snowy-grained photo of a woman. I haven't see this person in years, but I recognize her instantly. Fear starts flooding wildly through my body.

"Is this . . . is this Ellis?"

"Yes," my mother says. "She's living on the East Coast now. That picture was taken a couple of years ago when she renewed her driver's license."

I fold the paper in half so I don't have to see Ellis's eyes. "She looks just the same."

"She's working at some convenience store now," my mother says. "I'd love to be there when her life is finally interrupted, when the police arrest her for being an accessory to kidnapping."

The room starts to sway, and my mother doesn't even notice how I hold on to the table to keep my balance. "When will they arrest her?" I ask.

"Well, nothing will happen until we make a formal statement to the police. We'll have to wait until you're well enough to go back to California for a few days. Maybe we can take a long weekend once you've recovered and—"

"*Recovered?* I won't ever recover from what happened."

"No, I just mean that once you're stronger, once you're ready to talk to the police and district attorney—"

"You make it sound like prosecuting Ellis is the most important thing."

"Jamie, you're misunderstanding what I'm saying—"

"You shouldn't care about what happens to Ellis. You should care about what happened to *me*."

My mother looks she's been slapped across the face. "You *know* I care about what happened to you! You know that."

"How do I know that?"

Suddenly one of my mom's lawyer friends appears at the table. "Sorry to interrupt, Min, but we've run into a bit of a problem." He lowers his voice: "Can you come with me over to County? I just got a call from Sally Renfro; it sounds like she's in a bad way."

"Drew, no . . . what happened?"

"She's fragile, Min. We both know that. The stress of the trial's pushed her over the edge. She wants to see you."

"You'll have to handle it yourself," my mom says. "I need to spend some time with Jamie."

"Min—"

"I'm sorry, Drew. This is more important."

He starts to say something, then shakes his head, frustrated, and walks away.

My mom turns to me: "There isn't a day," she says softly, "there isn't a *minute* that goes by when I'm not thinking about what happened to you."

"But you don't know what it was like! You don't even have a clue!" The terror is back in full now, and I jump up from the table, knocking my chair over. I run for the door, push through the people who are waiting to be seated, then I'm outside and I don't know or care where I'm going; I'm just blindly walking.

"Jamie." My mother is at my side. She puts her hand on my arm and makes me stop walking; makes me stand still. "I want to know what it was like for you that night," she says. There are tears in her eyes. "Please, honey . . . please talk to me."

"Not here."

"Here," my mother says. "Right here, in the middle of the city. Here, on this crowded sidewalk. Tell me what it was like for you that night."

Without warning, the fury explodes inside me: "I stood there on the baseball field," I say, starting to cry, "and as soon as I saw him I knew something bad was going to happen. He dragged me off the field and there wasn't anything I could do! No one was there to protect me! I had to protect myself, and when the gun went off there was so much blood! There was so much blood . . . you can't know; you weren't there! I needed you to protect me and you weren't *there!* It's your fault! It's your *fault!*" The minute the terrible words are out of my mouth I want to wish them back. "Mom, I'm *sorry!* I didn't mean it! I didn't mean it!"

"Yes, you did," my mother says. She wraps her arms around me. "You meant it and it's all right, honey."

"No, it could have happened anytime! You couldn't be with me every single second."

"You're talking like a wise old lady of seventeen," my mother says. She wipes my face with her fingertips. "You were a little girl when it happened. Why *wouldn't* you be devastated I wasn't there to protect you? I'll never forgive myself for not being there, for not knowing about the terror you were going through."

"I never wanted you to feel bad. I never wanted that."

"You've had to live with the consequences of that night since you were nine," my mother says. "It's my turn to live with the guilt."

She takes my hand like she used to when I was little, and we start walking home. I see the picture so clearly now: I see myself at nine years old, trembling on the baseball field that night, then spinning Webb out of the deepest part of my imagination. He took care of me, looked after me, kept the anger and fear under lock and key. It's all been returned to me now, all those things that made me who I once was—all those things I had to leave behind one night on a baseball field when I was just nine years old.

38

MORGAN'S OVER FOR LUNCH A COUPLE
days later. She raves about my chicken Marsala;
has two helpings of it, in fact. I guess I'm getting
back in the swing of things, culinary-wise, at least.

"I want to show you something," I tell her
after I've cleared the table. I look through the
file my mom has started—the file with my name
on it—and find the picture of Ellis. I hand it to
Morgan.

"That's the girl who was my baby-sitter," I say.
"Ellis. I'm just now getting to the point where seeing her picture doesn't freak me out."

"Were you scared of her before—before it happened?"

"No, she was like a big sister to me. She'd paint
my toenails and take me shopping and tell me what
it felt like to be in love with someone."

"Was her boyfriend the one who . . ."

"The one who dragged me off the field. Yeah."

"God, what a betrayal."

"She had a cruel streak, and I never saw it, not
until the night I was kidnapped."

"What happens to her now?"

"We'll know after I talk to the police and district

attorney back in California. My mom and I thought we'd fly back over a weekend so she won't have to miss any of the trial."

"When are you going?"

"She's leaving it up to me. I'm just not sure I'm ready yet."

"You know something? It's really going to be hard for me when the Renfro trial ends and you go back home for good."

"Well, for me too," I say. "I mean, I finally find this great friend—to begin with, you actually *exist*—"

She laughs. "It's one of my best qualities."

The door to the apartment swings open, and my mom comes in. "Jamie?"

"Mom . . . how come you're home? Did court adjourn early today?"

"No, they're in afternoon session right now," she says. "Hi there, Morgan."

"Hi, Mrs. Tessman."

"Drew's going to be taking a more active part in the trial," my mom says, taking off her jacket. "It'll free me up to"—she looks at me—"it'll give me more time at home."

That's a shocker. "Really?" I say. "Well, have you had lunch? I still have some chicken Marsala left; I can heat it up."

"Sounds wonderful, darling."

I start for the kitchen. "Morgan, there's enough to go around if you want more."

She gets up from the table. "No, I have to get home, but thanks."

"Want to go to a movie or something tomorrow?"

"That'd be great," she says. "Call me, okay?"

"I will."

My mom follows me into the kitchen.

"Isn't this sort of a critical time in the trial?" I ask, adjusting the flame under the skillet. "I mean, what about Sally Renfro?"

"I'm not concerned about her," my mother says. "Drew's an excellent attorney." She reaches down and takes off her shoes. "What did you and Morgan do today?"

"Nothing spectacular, really. She showed me the theater school where she'll be going to college, then we walked over to Juice 'n' Java—did I tell you what happened there the other day?"

"What?" my mom asks.

I give the chicken Marsala a stir. "Some college guy asked if he could buy me a frappuccino. It was my very first coffee date, ta-da."

She smiles. "Did you have a good time?"

"I'm not sure. I was so nervous I don't even remember what we talked about."

"I can remember feeling that way on a date," my mom says. She sits down at the kitchen table. "It's nice to be asked, though, isn't it? Even if it's only for coffee."

I look at her. "Mom, what's this all about? I mean, you don't have to cut back on the trial because you're worried about me; I'm not going to flip out again."

"It's not that," she says. "I know it's cost you tremendously, everything that happened the night you were taken off the baseball field. I know it's interfered with every part of your life."

Seems my mom is full of surprises today. I know she's smart, but when did she get so perceptive?

"When I think about it," my mom says, "I realize you and I have been separated, in a way, ever since that night."

"I think so, too."

"I just wish—if only I'd gotten you some professional help years ago."

"You didn't know anything was wrong back then, Mom. Neither did I. It wasn't until you started working on the Renfro trial that all those hidden memory fragments began to surface. That's when I had my first clue that maybe the world I shared with Webb wasn't the same world I shared with everyone else."

She nods. "Why don't you forget about lunch for now, darling. Sit down and let's just talk, okay?"

I turn off the stove. "What do you want to talk about?"

"Tell me what it was like for you when you were in that other world."

"With Webb, you mean? Wow, where to start . . ."

"Just . . . start at the beginning," my mom says.

I sit down at the table. "Well, the first time I saw him was that night on the baseball field," I say. "After Ellis had driven away, Webb stepped out of the woods, and as soon as I saw him, I knew I was safe. I knew he'd always be around to protect me. . . ."

My mother is so attentive, it makes me want to open up the whole world to her, the world I had to keep secret for so many years.

It's sort of amazing, actually: Once I start talking to her, I just don't want to stop.

39

"MY MOM RAN AFTER ME WHEN I LEFT THE restaurant the other night," I tell the doctor, "and she let me stand there on the sidewalk and pour out everything I'd been holding back since that night on the baseball field. She just let me go ahead and . . . and—"

"Explode," the doctor says.

"Yeah," I say, laughing. "Explode."

"And the world didn't come to an end."

"No, sort of the opposite."

A thunderstorm's just started raging, and the office is growing dark—dark as night, almost. Rain slams against the windows, and the doctor gets up to turn on the desk lamp. It's just enough light to make the room feel cozy.

"It's like I've finally let my mom into my world," I say. "I've started talking to her. Really talking. That's something I couldn't ever do before."

The doctor comes back and sits in the chair facing mine. "When Webb became part of your life, he did more than just keep a secret for you," she says. "He also kept you from your mom."

"I know that now." I gaze out the windows and watch the dark clouds roll over the skyscrapers. I'm

glad I'm not outside in all that high wind and torren-
tial rain; I'm glad I made it here in time. Here where
it's safe. "I still miss him, though. It's scary to think of
going through life without ever seeing him again."

"You have someone in your life who can give
you a lot more than Webb could."

"My mom, you're talking about. Well, yeah.
She's been great. Did I tell you she's decided to cut
back her hours on the trial?"

"No." She tilts her head slightly and looks at
me. "What worries you about that?"

"When I first started coming here I thought I
could hide stuff from you. Now I don't even
bother trying. It's like you can read my mind."

She laughs. "No," she says. "I'm not clairvoy-
ant. But there are some things I'm good at, and
keeping my patients on track is one of them. So
tell me. What bothers you about your mom cutting back her hours?"

"I think she's doing it because of me."

"Why is that wrong?"

"I just feel sort of guilty about it. She's in the
middle of an important trial. Sally Renfro's depending on her."

"Your mom doesn't strike me as the type of
attorney who would put her client in jeopardy."

"I know, but . . ."

"Sally Renfro's not her daughter. You are."

Simple words, but they pack a punch. My eyes
fill with tears.

"This," the doctor says gently, "is part of the reality you never had with Webb." She hands me some Kleenex. "What you and your mom have is real. Constant. That makes it less painful, doesn't it, to surrender the fantasy?"

"It's just hard to let go."

"I know it is." She's quiet a moment, then: "Can you look back now and see who Webb really is?"

I take a deep breath, then I say it out loud for the first time: "I'm Webb."

"Yes."

"All the places Webb and I loved—the park, the beach, Otter Cove—my mom says those are places I used to visit with my dad. There are other things I remember about my dad that seem to fit Webb perfectly, and I was wondering . . . well, I don't believe in ghosts or angels or anything like that, but do you think—"

"Do I think Webb has an existence other than the unique one you created for him?" the doctor asks. "No. But you must have had enough memories of your dad to weave them into your life with Webb. That's worth knowing, isn't it?"

"I guess so. It's just such a huge struggle, this— whatever you want to call it—reentry into the real world."

"You've heard me say it before: It's going to take time."

"I know. I just wish there were a way to speed up the healing process."

She smiles. "So do I."

"My mom and I were talking about flying back to California sometime in the next few weeks so I can tell the police and the district attorney what happened."

"Is that something you want to do?"

"I don't know. I'm not sure yet. My mom says it might help me; she says it might give me a sense of control over what happened, control I haven't had since the night I was taken off the baseball field."

"I think your mom's right."

"We'd only be gone a few days, but I was wondering . . . could I call you from California if I needed to?"

"Of course."

There's something comforting about sitting here with the doctor in this dimly lit room while the rain pounds the windows. This is how I felt with Webb, only this time around I'm not worried that the feeling will vanish in a puff of blue smoke. A sensation of peace floats through me. "What happens when I have to leave here?" I ask. "When I leave for good, I mean. I'm not sure how I'm going to handle things . . . you know . . . without being able to come here. Without you."

"We'll know when the time is right to end your therapy," the doctor says. "It's a decision we'll make together, okay?"

I nod. "The thing is, I'm basically a coward. I'm not sure I'll ever be ready for real life."

"I'll let you in on a secret," the doctor says, a sly look in her eyes. "You're coping with real life right now. And you're doing it on your own. Without Webb."

It takes a moment for the revelation to sink in. "So maybe I'm handling things okay, then."

"No maybe about it, Jamie. You've accomplished a hell of a lot. You know that, don't you?"

"Yes." I look at her and smile. "I remember feeling like this when I learned to ride my bike. My mom ran along beside me, holding on to the bike until I got enough momentum, then all of a sudden I looked down and realized I was zooming along on my own power."

"You were flying," the doctor says. "Like now."

"Just like now," I say. "Flying . . ."

40

"CHANNEL SEVEN'S DOING A REPORT ON the Renfro trial," Morgan says.

"Yeah, I'm watching it while I pack." I cradle the phone against my shoulder while I fold one of my T-shirts. "It's the same footage they run whenever there's nothing new to report."

"How much longer before the trial's over?" Morgan asks.

"A month, at least, my mom says."

"Jamie?" my mom calls from the bedroom. "Have you seen my briefcase?"

"Hold on a sec," I say into the phone. "Mom, it's here on the coffee table."

"What?"

"It's on the coffee table!" I yell.

"Hey, you're giving me severe ear trauma," Morgan says.

"Sorry. I have an appointment with your aunt at two. Want to get something to eat afterward?"

"I won't be at the office this afternoon; I have to go to an orientation over at school," she says. "It'll have to be later, okay?"

"Don't forget: we leave for the airport at five."

"Jamie?" my mom calls. "I couldn't hear you,

darling. Did you say my briefcase is out there?"

"I'd better go," I tell Morgan. "See you later."

"I understand," she says. "It's so hard getting a little one ready for the day—"

"Definitely."

My mom walks into the living room just as I'm hanging up the phone. "Jamie, have you seen—"

"Your briefcase, Mom, is here on the coffee table."

"Ah, thank you," she says. She glances at the TV. "Not another recap of the trial . . ."

"It's the same stuff they keep showing. I think they need a new angle on the story."

"Well, they'll have one in a few weeks when we turn the case over to the jury."

"Do you think Sally Renfro will be acquitted?"

"I hope so, darling." She drops some papers into her briefcase. "I don't want you to think your case is the same as hers, though. It's not. You won't be charged with what happened after you were kidnapped off the baseball field."

I know my case isn't the same as Sally Renfro's, yet her trial is what caused my inner world to disintegrate this summer. No telling how messed up I'd be if that world had stayed buried.

"Drew's going to take us to the airport, so we'll swing by here after court adjourns. You can ask the doorman to help you with the suitcases."

"One suitcase is enough for both of us, don't you think?" I ask. "We're only going to be gone a few days, and we have clothes at the house."

"I'm glad at least one of us knows what she's doing." She gives me a kiss, then heads for the door. "I'll see you later, darling."

When I think of my mom, I think of perpetual motion.

"So," the doctor says. "Tomorrow you and your mother talk to the police?"

"Unless I fall completely apart."

"I don't think that will happen."

"It's overwhelming, though, when I think of everything that's ahead. I mean, eventually Ellis will be brought back to California to face kidnapping charges, and I'm just not sure how I'll handle it when I have to see her again—"

"Jamie," the doctor says. "Let's just take it one step at a time, okay?"

"I know." I lean back in my chair. "Have I been your worst patient? There were times I was so awful to you; I don't see how you even put up with me."

"I like challenges," she says, then, looking closely at me, "What is it?"

"It's going to seem strange to be back home without Webb. The last time I was at Otter Cove I was still living in the clouds, so to speak, and Webb was at my side. I'm not sure I'm going to like being so . . . earthbound."

"It's really the best place to be, though, isn't it?" the doctor asks. "It's where your mom is, where you made a friend, where you finally gained the strength to break out of a world that was keeping you from leading a full life—"

"You're like a tour guide for reality," I say, and she laughs.

"I have a feeling you'll get through tomorrow just fine." She glances at her watch. "Looks like our time's up, so I'll see you next week, all right?"

She walks me to the door and out into the waiting room.

"Dr. Hackett? I want to give you something." Before I left the apartment, I slipped one of my seashells into my backpack, and now I fumble around till I find it. "It's a sand dollar," I say, handing her the little cracked shell. "I used to think Webb gave it to me, but I guess . . . well, now I know I was really alone when I found it."

"It's beautiful," she says, closing her fingers around it. She smiles at me. "Thank you, Jamie."

I give her a quick hug, then turn around and run down the hall, one step at a time, not looking back.

Not looking back at all.

41

ONLY A FEW MINUTES TILL WE BOARD OUR plane, but my mom's on her cell phone with one of her lawyer pals, rattling off some last-minute thoughts about the trial. It makes me smile, sort of, because even though I'm her daughter, I've finally decided that the Renfro trial is her baby. I think it's hard for her to leave it, even if it's only for a weekend. She's always going to be a bit obsessed with her work—that's just who she is—but we're not disconnected like we once were, back when Webb was the focus of my life.

I tap my mother on the shoulder. "Mom, are you almost through? All of the pay phones are tied up, and I want to call Morgan before we leave. She wasn't home when I tried to call earlier."

"I'll just be a couple more minutes," she says, and I sigh and turn around and watch some of the other travelers as they hurry through the airport. It's while I'm standing here people-watching that it suddenly occurs to me: I don't feel set apart from the rest of the world anymore. When did that happen? Maybe it's my reward for completing the reality tour, a tour I didn't even know I'd be taking when I landed here in this modern Oz.

"Jamie!"

In the old days, I'd expect it to be Webb, but I'm earthbound now, and it's not Webb, but Morgan, who's hurrying down the concourse.

"I was afraid I wouldn't make it," she says. She's flushed and breathless from her race-walk through the airport. "I lost track of the time at that orientation thing."

"You came all the way out to the airport just to say good-bye?" I ask. "How'd you know where to find us?"

"Well, here's the interesting part," Morgan says, holding up an airline ticket. "I'm not here to say good-bye. Your mom invited me to California for the weekend."

My mom's still on the phone, but she smiles at me and nods.

"We wanted it to be a surprise," Morgan says. "So, are you? Surprised, I mean."

"Don't I *look* surprised?"

"You look stunned."

"I *am* stunned."

"I can't wait to get to California. The first thing I want to do is see those killer otters you were telling me about."

"Hope you brought some athletic shoes," I say. "You can't climb down the rocks in the cove if you're wearing skinny little sandals like those."

"We have to climb down *rocks* to see the otters? What kinds of rocks?"

"Big ones."

"Well, is there a handrail or something to hang on to while we climb down?"

"Handrail! Wow, you really *are* an urban princess, aren't you?"

"Okay, so I've led a sheltered life!" She digs in her backpack and pulls out a couple of candy bars. "Here," she says, handing me a Snickers. "I brought along my stash of chocolate."

"What—afraid they only have health food in California?"

"I just didn't want to take any chances."

I peel the wrapper off my candy bar. "Hey, did I ever thank you for butting into my life and getting me help when I needed it?"

"No," Morgan says. "You were damn unhappy about it, as a matter of fact."

"Okay, well, I'm thanking you now."

She looks at me and grins. "You're welcome."

"I'm glad you're coming back with us."

"So am I," she says.

It's not so bad, actually, being earthbound like everyone else. No more mind slips: I know exactly what lies ahead—well, some of it, at least. In just a little while my mom and Morgan and I will be on our way to California, then tomorrow I'll meet with the police and tell them what happened to me one night when I was only nine years old. I think maybe I'll get through it all right. My mom will be with me, and it helps a lot knowing Morgan's going to be around this weekend. Whatever else the future holds is kind of murky, but that doesn't stop me from dreaming of the life I want. An ordinary life filled with extraordinary things is what I wish for, a life that picks up where it left off that night on the baseball field, a life filled with the everyday magic of friends and wonder and love and laughter. These are some of the things I hope will be waiting for me in the future—a future that begins just a few hours from now, as soon as our plane lands in California and we touch down on the other side of the rainbow.

JULIE REECE DEAVER grew up in Glen Ellyn, Illinois. She is the author of several novels, including *Say Goodnight, Gracie,* an ALA Best Book for Young Adults, which introduced two of the characters featured in *The Night I Disappeared*. Deaver has worked as a teacher's aide in special education and started her writing career in television comedy. She is an artist as well as a writer; her illustrations have appeared in *The New Yorker, Reader's Digest,* and *The Chicago Tribune*. She lives on the Monterey Peninsula in California with her blue-eyed cat, Lincoln Rhyme. Readers are welcome to contact her at JulieDeaver@aol.com.

Three teens face the ultimate challenge of their lives in these inspiring stories of hope, courage, and love.

Deborah Kent

Why Me?

THE COURAGE TO LIVE
No one could have prepared her for what lay ahead...

Diagnosed with lupus, Chloe Peterson is suddenly fighting for her life—against the greatest enemy of all: herself. . . .

LIVING WITH A SECRET
How long could she hide the truth?

When Cassie Mullins takes a job as a counselor at a camp for diabetic children, her parents think she will be safe. There's only one problem: Cassie doesn't want to be a drag with the other counselors, and she is the only one who is diabetic. So she decides to keep it a secret.

DON'T CRY FOR YESTERDAY
All it took was a reckless date. . . .

Amber Novak's life has changed forever. Suddeny, her plans to be a singer in a newly formed rock band seem impossible. A date with hunky Eric Moore ended in a car crash, and Amber will never walk again. Her dreams have never seemed farther away. How can she find the courage to rebuild her life and dare to dream again?

Available from Simon & Schuster

William Corlett's

THE MAGICIAN'S HOUSE QUARTET

Thirteen-year-old William Constant and his two younger sisters, Mary and Alice, have come to ancient, mysterious Golden House in Wales for the holidays. Their lives will never be the same once they enter the Magician's House—and discover their destiny.

THE STEPS UP THE CHIMNEY

*What evil lurks in Golden House?
The children know. . . .*

THE DOOR IN THE TREE

*It's even more dangerous when
the magic is real. . .*

THE TUNNEL BEHIND THE WATERFALL

All that glitters . . .

THE BRIDGE IN THE CLOUDS

Magic can be dangerous . . .

Available from Simon & Schuster

Beware cheerleaders bearing gifts....

NIGHT OF THE POMPON
Sarah Jett

Pompons aren't just for pep rallies any more....

Who knows what evil lies beyond the oven door? Jendra MacKenzie knows—it's a strangely powerful pompon that turns bright-eyed cheerleaders into gray-eyed monsters. But what she doesn't know is how to explain the unusual events unfolding at the Davy Crockett school ever since ultra-popular Tina Shepard handed her a coyote head and made her the cheerleading mascot. Who's responsible for the sudden disappearance of the last mascot, and the principal's pants...and the principal?

When Jendra searches for answers, she finds nothing but trouble. Propelled by powers she can't control, she winds up disco dancing on top of her desk, flying to a faraway dentist's office, and dodging falling eighth-graders in the second story girls' bathroom. If this trend toward the bizarre continues, she might even pass pre-algebra...unless the cheerleaders have something more sinister in mind....

**Available from
Simon & Schuster**